Scandal's Daughter

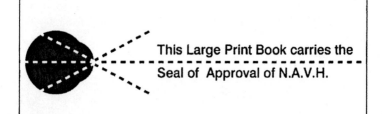

This Large Print Book carries the
Seal of Approval of N.A.V.H.

Scandal's Daughter

Phylis Ann Warady

Thorndike Press • Waterville, Maine

Published in 2005 by arrangement with Phylis Warady.

Thorndike Press® Large Print Romance.

The tree indicium is a trademark of Thorndike Press.

The text of this Large Print edition is unabridged.
Other aspects of the book may vary from the original edition.

Set in 16 pt. Plantin by Liana M. Walker.

Printed in the United States on permanent paper.

Library of Congress Cataloging-in-Publication Data

Warady, Phylis Ann.
    Scandal's daughter / Phylis Ann Warady.
        p. cm.
    ISBN 0-7862-7224-4 (lg. print : hc : alk. paper)
    1. Inheritance and succession — Fiction. 2. Women
music teachers — Fiction. 3. Scandals — Fiction.
4. Large type books. I. Title.
PS3573.A65S24 2005
813′.54—dc22   2004058596

This book is dedicated to dear friends,
Dorothy and Norman Daniels,
who first suggested
that the author write a Regency.
P.A.W.

As the Founder/CEO of NAVH, the only national health agency solely devoted to those who, although not totally blind, have an eye disease which could lead to serious visual impairment, I am pleased to recognize Thorndike Press* as one of the leading publishers in the large print field.

Founded in 1954 in San Francisco to prepare large print textbooks for partially seeing children, NAVH became the pioneer and standard setting agency in the preparation of large type.

Today, those publishers who meet our standards carry the prestigious "Seal of Approval" indicating high quality large print. We are delighted that Thorndike Press is one of the publishers whose titles meet these standards. We are also pleased to recognize the significant contribution Thorndike Press is making in this important and growing field.

Lorraine H. Marchi, L.H.D.
Founder/CEO
NAVH

* Thorndike Press encompasses the following imprints: Thorndike, Wheeler, Walker and Large Print Press.

Author's note: The scandal referred to in *Scandal's Daughter* is based on an actual tragic affair involving the Earl of Sandwich, First Lord of the Admiralty, Martha Ray, a gifted singer, and Captain James Hackman. While I've taken license with the actual date and softened Martha's character to suit the genre, the Earl of Sandwich did live openly with Martha, who was as much his prodigy as she was his mistress. Furthermore, their daughter married well, despite the scandal that rocked all of London society at the time it occurred.

— P.A.W.

Chapter 1

"Why so glum, Agnes? I should think you'd be in transports after receiving Lord Devonwych's message," observed Sarah Butler.

Agnes Pixley, headmistress of a fashionable ladies' seminary in Kent, stopped squinting at the astonishing letter that had come in the post to peer myopically at her first cousin's daughter. "I know I should, Sarah. I keep telling myself I must be happy, if only for Diantha's sake, but . . ."

"I confess I don't understand you," Miss Butler confided. "His lordship's unexpected summons is an answer to your prayers. With her penchant for mischief, Diantha Fraser has been a thorn in your side ever since you felt obliged to engage her as music teacher."

"You malign the child unjustly. She is an excellent instructress, and you must own her musical talents are remarkable. Besides, I had no other choice. The letter I received in response to the one I wrote to her father, advising him that his natural daughter was ready to leave the schoolroom, instructed me to find her a suitable post."

"No doubt Lord Devonwych considered his obligation discharged upon completion of her education. 'Tis a cruel world, cousin."

"Very true! Unfortunately, both her youth and her beauty made it impossible for me to comply with his request. Fashionable young matrons with young children do not wish to compete with a winsome governess for their husband's attentions, whereas the elder mamas would consider Diantha too tempting a morsel to dangle before their stripling sons. But what man understands that?"

So Miss Pixley had ignored inner qualms and engaged Miss Fraser as the school's musical instructress, drawing what comfort she could from the girl's rich contralto voice — the envy of the neighbourhood at Sunday chapel — while doing her best not to dwell overly much on Diantha's lively spirits.

A light scratching upon the study door cut short the headmistress's musings. "That will be Miss Fraser come in answer to my summons."

10

The headmistress waited until her cousin quit the room before issuing a gruff command to enter. The door widened to allow nineteen-year-old Diantha Fraser to step inside. As usual, Miss Pixley experienced a tug on her heartstrings, for the sight of her former pupil attired in serviceable brown wool filled her with sad resignation.

"You wish to see me, ma'am?" Diantha's voice was slightly husky, tinged with curiosity, yet melodious.

"I do. Kindly oblige me by closing the door and taking a chair."

Diantha sat on a plain wooden chair, vainly attempting to tuck a recalcitrant tendril of raven-black hair into the coiled knot at the base of her neck. She looked expectantly at Miss Pixley.

"I have splendid news, child. Your father is not well and wishes to see you."

To the elder woman's dismay, Diantha's rosy complexion blanched. Miss Pixley bit her tongue.

"What a bubblehead I am! I should have broken it to you gradually. Would you like some vinaigrette?"

"No, ma'am. I'll be myself in a trice."

"To be sure. How fortunate your father has fallen ill. Dear me, that's not what I mean precisely. What I meant to say is how nice that he wishes to receive you at last."

"Fiddle! It is only his nagging conscience, I daresay. No matter. I've not the least intention of indulging his whim."

It was Miss Pixley's turn to go pale. Indeed, the vehemence smoldering in Miss Fraser's eyes caused the hairs to stiffen on the back of the headmistress's scrawny neck.

"Have a care, miss! Must I remind you he is your father? A nobleman too! He deserves your respect."

"Does he? Why?"

Miss Pixley's tone was as repressive as Diantha's had been impudent. "I had no idea you harboured such resentment against that excellent man. I must say your attitude is not the least bit becoming."

In a cold fury, Diantha retorted, "You can hardly expect me to fly into transports because my *father* has finally consented to receive me. Need I remind you, he washed his hands of me when I turned eighteen?"

The headmistress shook her head. "Poor misguided innocent. Useless to rail at the world, you know. I don't mean to refine overmuch upon it, but given your circumstance of birth, you are quite fortunate to have been educated. That's to your father's credit, particularly in light of the cloud surrounding your mother's death."

"Cloud? What cloud?" Diantha asked, obviously intrigued.

Miss Pixley looked stricken. "It is not my place to enlighten you."

Diantha took a deep breath and straightened her spine. "With all due respect, Miss Pixley, I am a grown woman and have been earning my keep for the past year. Surely I have a right to know."

"So you do. All the more reason you should pay your father a visit. He's the proper person to ask, not me."

A look of bleakness stole into the young girl's face as bits and pieces of fragmented memory came rushing back. Beautiful Mama, dressed for the opera, bending to brush a soft kiss on her cheek. It had been the last time she'd seen her. For that matter, after that night she'd scarcely seen dearest Papa, who'd barricaded himself in his own suite and, according to kitchen gossip, had refused to emerge — even for Mama's funeral.

Without warning, Diantha was seized with an intense longing for the loving security she'd lost so inexplicably shortly after her eighth birthday. Her vision blurred.

Miss Pixley clucked sympathetically. "Have a good cry, child. I daresay you will have ample time to pack your trunk before his lordship's coach arrives on the door-step."

Brushing away tears with an angry swipe, Diantha leapt to her feet. "But, ma'am, after his shabby treatment, I don't wish to go to my father. I prefer to make my own way in the world."

Frustrated, the headmistress wrung her hands. "Diantha Fraser, that's outside of enough! For all you know, he's on his deathbed. Surely you are not so hard-hearted that you'd refuse a dying man's last wish."

Her young charge gripped the arms of her chair so hard her knuckles whitened. Her voice flat with despair, she said, "I've the right of it now. What with my lamen-table tendency to become involved in girlish pranks, you wish me gone. Only please, ma'am, let me stay. I give you my solemn word to reform."

Miss Pixley's face softened as under-standing dawned. She threw her bony arms about the troubled young woman. "No such thing! I will own you try my patience at times, but I've no wish to be rid of you. All I want is what is best for you. My wish for each of my pupils."

"Then I may stay on?" Diantha's grey eyes anxiously scanned the elder woman's face.

"Go to your father, child. Afterward, should you wish to return here, I shall be most happy to receive you."

Again bleak despair dominated Diantha's features. Rising, the young woman sighed. "I must go, then?"

"It is the wisest course," Miss Pixley advised gently.

Diantha was half way to the door before she whirled about. "What of Miss Stracey's voice lesson? I should be with her directly."

The headmistress issued a wintry smile. "I believe it may be safely cancelled. Indeed, I never imagined you would turn her into a songbird."

A shaky chuckle escaped Diantha. "Very true! Poor widgeon cannot carry a tune in a bucket! But I know you need every shilling you can lay your hands on to keep this establishment running. Far be it for me to ever throw a spoke in your wheel."

As usual, Diantha's candour was accompanied by an innocent smile. The combination never failed to beguile Miss Pixley. Nevertheless, she felt obliged to deliver a mild rebuke. "Mind your saucy tongue, miss!"

Too far away to see the twinkle in the headmistress's eye, Diantha murmured contritely, "Indeed, ma'am, I beg your pardon."

The clock chimed thrice as Sebastian Pemborough, Sixth Marquess of Ravistock, carried the dozing noblewoman across the entry hall and up the carpeted stairs. Entering Lady Fitzwilliam's boudoir, he noted the candles were now guttering in their sockets. With infinite care, he placed her on the bed, then gazed at her tousled mass of red-gold curls, at her alabaster skin, slightly flushed at the cheeks. Asleep, Honoria looked positively angelic; awake, she was capable of giving the devil a run for his money.

Ravistock's lips twitched. Not that he meant to complain. Her ladyship might be a spoilt little schemer, accustomed to bending all men who crossed her path to her will, but on the plus side of the ledger, she was a perfect pocket Venus. Even more gratifying, Ravistock found her to be passionate, a rarity in the upper circles of society, despite the tendency of neglected aristocratic wives to acquire a lover —

once they'd provided their husband with an heir.

Honoria's eyelids fluttered open and she asked, "What time is it?"

"After three, my lovely. Time we parted."

"But we just arrived. Must you go? Henry seldom gets in before dawn," she coaxed softly.

"Even so, we must be discreet. If I linger, I may be seen leaving. I've no wish to blemish your reputation."

"Bother my reputation!" Lady Fitzwilliam exclaimed, reshaping cherry red lips into a pout.

Sebastian's sudden surge of impatience surprised him. Usually he found her womanly wiles enchanting. Usually he didn't mind that this lovely morsel — with a scant twenty summers in her dish — had no more brains than a peahen. As he started to edge discreetly toward the door, her eyes glittered like emeralds and she gave him one of her most enticing smiles.

"Do you know what I wish?" she asked.

Ravistock shook his head. Honoria was a lovely creature but her wilfulness was beginning to pall. "Suppose you tell me."

"I wish you and I would sail away to Italy and live in a villa. Just imagine,

Sebastian. No more having to leave my bed in the middle of the night. Come morning, we'd wake in each other's arms. Best of all, we need not concern ourselves with what the *ton* thinks."

"Fly to Italy?" He gave an ungentlemanly snort. "Pray don't be a goose! Such a course would be certain to ruin you. This is not going to happen. Not if I have anything to say about it," Ravistock asserted with pardonable firmness.

At this juncture, Honoria's abigail burst into the room. Lady Fitzwilliam glared at her maid. "What is the meaning of this intrusion, Nan?"

"Oh, ma'am, I fear you are undone. Sir Henry's downstairs. Drunk as a lord, he is! Yelling to the top of his lungs. He's coming up here!"

"Angels defend us!" cried Lady Fitzwilliam.

Sebastian laughed sardonically. Bad enough that he'd cuckolded Sir Henry. He had no wish to compound his transgression by killing the man. Should it come to a duel, he would have to delope. And Sir Henry, that silly young cawker, was a crack shot. Sebastian had no wish to die. His wisest course, it seemed, was to avoid the confrontation entirely.

"Calm yourself, Honoria," he commanded, tossing the abigail a guinea. "Go you below-stairs, Nan, and do your best to stall him."

"Gladly, my lord. I make no doubt Biggers could use a hand. The master was carrying on something fierce when I slipped upstairs to warn milady."

"Off with you, then, Nan! There's a good girl!"

The instant the door closed, Honoria said, "What good will it do to stall him? Sooner or later, he's bound to come here and then I'm undone."

"Not, madam, if you stop prattling and allow me to leave by way of the balcony."

Honoria clapped her hands. "I'd forgotten you used to climb up the drainpipe at first. So romantic!"

"Farewell, sweetling," Sebastian called as he swung off the balcony and caught hold of a sturdy elm branch.

Several hours later, inside the Earl of Devonwych's town house overlooking Cavendish Square, the ailing peer's housekeeper gently jostled his shoulder. "My lord, are you awake?"

His lordship had been dozing, but now he came to his senses with a start. "What do you want, Crawford?"

"The Marquess of Ravistock is come. You bade me to rouse you the instant he appeared."

"So I did. Show him up."

Though stout-hearted, Mrs. Crawford hesitated. While the present Earl of Devonwych had ever been plagued with a ghostly pallor, of late his pale white skin had taken on a greyish cast that she could not like.

"Quit dawdling, woman. Get Ravistock. It's imperative I speak to him."

"Pray don't excite yourself, my lord. I'll fetch him directly."

Minutes later, Mrs. Crawford returned with his visitor. "The Marquess of Ravistock, my lord," she announced before she withdrew.

"Appreciate your promptness, Sebastian," said Devonwych.

"Not at all, sir," the marquess replied politely.

Truth be told, he'd barely completed his toilet before the footman had come with the earl's note. He'd been looking forward to a large breakfast. Instead, he'd settled for a cup of coffee and a roll, much to his protesting stomach's displeasure.

Sebastian was quite fond of the earl,

who'd had the kindness to take him under his wing when he'd first joined the Admiralty staff. It was common knowledge that his mentor was gravely ill. Thus, he'd felt it only prudent to answer his summons immediately.

"How may I serve you, my lord?"

"I've a favor I would ask of you."

"If it's within my power, I'm at your service."

"Minute I laid eyes on you, I knew you were a right one!" The earl waved a frail arm towards a sealed letter lying on the night table. "Take that with you when you leave. Mind you don't read it until after I'm gone."

"You have my word, sir. Anything else?"

"I've sent for my natural daughter, Diantha. Shipped her off to school in Kent when her mother died. Want to see her comfortably settled before I cock up my toes."

"Admirable sentiment, sir. However, I fail to see what you need me for."

"Want you to keep an eye on Richmond. Though he's my son and heir, never could stand him. I know it's presumptuous to ask, but I need someone to protect her from his malicious streak."

"I'll do what I can, but you must understand I've no authority over him."

Devonwych sighed. "Even so, my honour compels me to ask. Least I can do for the chit after neglecting her all these years. If I know Richmond, he'll try to turn her out of the house the minute I die. She's to stay on through the funeral. However, it's after the will is read that has me worried. Richmond'll be mad as a hatter. Don't let him use Diantha as a scapegoat."

"Never fear. I shall hover nearby until after the reading of the will. Does that ease your mind, sir?"

"Yes, it does. Now that our business is done, allow me to congratulate you for succeeding to your father's title."

"Thank you, sir. The honour was wholly unexpected. Father was in sound health."

"Just so. Who would have thought he'd be cut down on the hunting field? Bloody shame! But then, none of us know for certain when it is our turn, do we?"

"No, indeed." The marquess's eyes narrowed pensively. "I fear the estates my father left me are in sorry shape. Though I'm by no means a pauper, thanks to a legacy received from my mother's side of the family, I still see no way to bring them up to snuff at present."

"Take my advice, my boy, marry an

heiress. That way you can repair the family coffers depleted by your scapegrace father. High time you settled down and set up your nursery."

"Nursery? I'm only six and twenty."

"I daresay it's presumptuous of me to tell you how to go on, but frankly I don't like your dalliance with Lady Fitzwilliam. You may want to consider changing course before you embroil yourself in a scandal. Speaking from experience, there is nothing so devastating. Think on it, lad, think on it."

"I promise I will. Now I'd best go. You look worn to the bone."

"By all means take yourself off. Mind you, don't forget to take my letter along."

"No danger of that, sir." Sebastian picked it up and slipped it into an inside pocket of his coat.

Devonwych watched Ravistock stroll across the room in long easy strides, and just as the marquess crossed the threshold, the earl muttered softly, "Good-bye and Godspeed."

Chapter 2

The abrupt halt of Lord Devonwych's well-sprung travel coach aroused Diantha from a fitful doze. Yawning, she tested prickly limbs before peering out the isinglass at a neat Georgian house overlooking Cavendish Square.

As she gazed at the arched entrance flanked on either side by tall windows, adorned with flower boxes of red geraniums, a rush of emotion brought a searing lump to her throat. Of course, she had not the least intention of giving way to tears, but, after all, this was her first glimpse in many years of the elegant establishment which, as a child, she'd regarded as her home.

Diantha's thoughts scattered as Timothy, the young footman, let down the steps. Grateful for his bring support, she smiled her thanks.

Blushing to the roots of his hair, the footman tugged at the gold-trimmed collar of his dark-blue livery and volunteered in a breathless rush, "If I may be so bold as to drop a 'int in your ear, miss, 'iggins, milord's 'igh-in-the-instep butler, is 'overing at the front door and 'e don't like to be kept cooling 'is 'eels."

Duty discharged, Timothy scrambled up beside Rhoades, the coachman, who jerked the reins smartly, setting the yoked bays in motion. Diantha watched the travel-stained coach lumber round the bend. Then, having no further excuse to dawdle, she approached the front door. However, before she could raise the carved lion's-head knocker, the door was opened by a tall, rigid figure, wearing an expression of haughty impatience.

"You must be Higgins," she observed.

He executed a stiff bow before venturing with chilly reserve, "And you, I presume, are Miss Fraser."

"Indeed I am. I understand my father is expecting me."

"So I've been informed. No doubt you will wish to change your dress before you visit his bedside."

Diantha flushed. *Toplofty creature!* It was not the suggestion itself that raised her hackles but, rather, his condescending manner that rankled.

"Ah, here is his lordship's housekeeper, come to take you up to your bedchamber," he intoned, looking down his beak of a nose. "Once you are ready, she will escort you to the library. Before you see his lordship, Viscount Richmond desires a word with you."

Basil Richmond. Her half brother.

"Can that not be postponed until after I've seen my father?"

Higgins looked affronted by her presumptuousness. "Lord Richmond is in charge of the household during his father's illness." The air of finality in his voice made further argument futile.

As the only son, Richmond stood to inherit both the title and the estates. Even so, his authority over his father's affairs surprised her. She retained the impression from her childhood that father and son did not get along. Either her memory had played her false, or else in the ensuing years their relationship had undergone a dramatic change. Whatever the case, it would be churlish to refuse her brother's request. Besides, his reason for summoning her might be important.

"Crawford, would you be so good as to escort Miss Fraser to her room," Higgins intoned.

Crawfy? Her childhood nanny? Surely not! Diantha spun round, a rush of affection surging through her as she recognized the housekeeper. She was about to call out a greeting and fling her arms around the sturdy woman when Crawford's intent gaze stopped her.

"Follow me, miss," Crawford said without a flicker of warmth.

They went up the carpeted stairs at a demure pace. At the upper landing, the housekeeper veered right, walked the length of a dim passage, and flung open a door. Obeying the woman's gesture, Diantha stepped into a room of delicate French furnishings displayed against apple-green walls. Rich velvet draperies tinted a deep rose were sashed with gold cording to allow the late-afternoon sun to filter through filmy panels of organza. About to voice her pleasure in the cheerful surroundings, she was distracted by the housekeeper's sigh.

"Whew!" Crawford leaned back against the closed door. "For a second or two below-stairs, I feared you'd let the cat out of the bag. Thanks be to God you had the sense to keep your tongue between your teeth."

Diantha laughed. "As if I'd dare! Well I

remember from nursery days what a scold you'd deliver, should I choose to ignore that dampening look!"

She enveloped the housekeeper in a warm hug.

"No need to squeeze the life out of me," Crawford complained, feigning crossness.

Puzzlement dominated Diantha's soft features as she asked, "Why, Crawfy? Why should it matter if anyone knows you were once my nanny?"

"Viscount Richmond engaged Higgins. I see no reason to let him know you've an ally in the house. Make no mistake that muckworm's in your brother's pocket. Besides, Richmond has been casting about for an excuse to dismiss me. Without a character, I vow!"

"I collect my half brother has taken you in dislike?"

"Much I care!" Crawford huffed. "I've detested him ever since he was a grubby schoolboy bent on torturing you whenever my back was turned. Though I cannot be certain he recalls me, as his visits were as rare as hen's teeth. Until lately, he ain't seen me for years, and what with my hair turning grey between times, he mayn't see me as was once your nanny. But that is neither here nor there. There's much you should know."

Diantha's interest quickened. Crawford looked positively grim, she decided.

"Your brother used your father's failing health as an excuse to worm his way into the household. Then two weeks ago, he had to go away for several days.

"While Richmond was gone, the earl got better. I was that surprised when he asked for pen and paper and writ a letter in his own hand, calling you to his bedside. After franking it, he bade me post it at once — which I did. When Richmond returned and got wind of the scheme, he tried to get back the coach sent to fetch you, but it was too late."

Diantha frowned. "I cannot understand why Basil should object to my visit? More than likely, my father merely wishes to clear his conscience by making peace with me before he dies. No doubt he'll order me back to Kent afterwards, so why kick up such a dust? Or does Basil think it's not quite the thing because of my irregular birth?"

"You know you're baseborn, then?"

Diantha nodded. "The headmistress of the seminary I attended felt I should know when she offered me a post."

"Wise of her, I must own. As to Richmond, he's ever been a prude." Crawford's words were saturated with scorn. "But that's not the whole of it. If you ask me, his reason for trying to prevent your seeing your father is greed."

"I confess I am completely in the dark. What do I have that he could possibly covet?"

" 'Tis not what you have, but what you may inherit that worries him. He fears his lordship may take a notion to leave you some money."

"I doubt it would be a significant sum. Why begrudge me a pittance when he stands to inherit all of the entailed estate?"

"The gossipmongers say he's squandered his wife's fortune and hasn't a feather to fly with. It's my belief his creditors have run him to ground here in Cavendish Square. He seldom leaves the house until dusk, except on Sunday, when they cannot touch him. Too risky to venture abroad during the daylight hours, I make no doubt. If he's clamped in debtor's prison, it won't set too well with his shrew of a wife."

Diantha knit her brow, deep in thought. "He gambles, then?"

"Not like he did in his salad days. Mind, he's not turned over a new leaf. More's the pity. He gambles less because he can't raise the ready. 'Tis my thought he's hoping to inherit all of his father's blunt, including unentailed funds to settle the worst of his debts and to dower those two gawky daughters when they're old enough to make their bow."

The housekeeper broke off as a chambermaid entered bearing a can of hot water. Immediately after her arrived two footmen struggling with Diantha's trunk, followed by Timothy carrying her portmanteau. Crawford asked to be allowed to help her change, but Diantha firmly refused.

Alone, Diantha shook off her weariness. After bathing her hands and face, she brushed the tangles from her silky, blue-black hair and arranged it in a neat coil at the base of her neck. She inspected her brown serge dress with critical eyes, removing a bit of lint from her sleeve. Her travel attire had held up remarkably well, though it now exuded a tired, dejected air. However, she didn't wish to waste precious minutes changing to another gown. She wanted to get the interview with her father over with, for the anticipated ordeal had weighed heavily upon her during her journey. And there was Basil to deal with as well. Best to go and learn firsthand how things stood between her half brother and herself.

Descending the stairs, she went to the library, where a light scratching on the door brought a snarled invitation to enter. Inside a room crammed with heavy mahogany pieces and lit only by a single candle and a fire flickering upon the grate, she watched her brother, seated behind her father's desk, who continued to write as though oblivious of her presence.

Unexpectedly, she experienced a sharp ache in her chest, for Basil's pale countenance vividly recalled to mind her father. Evidently, as her brother aged, he began to bear a remarkable resemblance to his sire.

Indeed, at first glance, she had thought it was Papa seated at his desk, rather than Basil, and a wave of affection had engulfed her. This surprised her, because she'd sincerely believed she'd hardened her heart towards the earl when he'd written to Miss Pixley in Kent to advise he felt his obligation to his baseborn daughter ended with the completion of her education.

Stifling anger engendered by memories of his hurtful rejection, Diantha firmly returned her mind to her present situation. Not one to suffer in silence, the fact that her brother was deliberately ignoring her propelled her forwards.

"I understand you wish a word with me before I see Papa," she said, sitting down in a chair near Basil.

As Richmond lifted his gaze, she saw that the whites of his eyes held a pinkish tinge. It seemed he'd imbibed too freely from the decanter of brandy resting by his hand.

Jabbing the quill into a vacant hole in the inkstand, he regarded her with a knowing smirk. "Miss . . . Fraser, I presume?"

Obviously, Basil did not wish to acknowledge the connection. So be it, Diantha thought, repelled by his grimy unkempt fingernails drumming upon the arm of her chair.

"I had hoped you would take time to change into a more suitable gown. Surely you don't mean to see his lordship looking like a dowd," he sneered.

Nettled by his audacity in criticizing her appearance, particularly when he was so careless of his own, she almost let loose of her impulsive tongue, but managed to refrain. Obviously, Basil wished to provoke her into a quarrel, and she wasn't about to let him bait her.

"Not that it matters. I have decided not to permit you to see him. Father's health is too precarious to allow a bedside reunion. You have my permission to spend the night. Tomorrow I suggest you board the mail coach for Kent."

She threw him a look of dry amusement. "Really, brother mine, I must ask you not to concern yourself with my affairs. In any case, I do not have the necessary funds."

"If that's all that's keeping you, I shall gladly pay the shot."

"Indeed, I know you wish me to the devil, but what on earth makes you think I shall meekly oblige? I have not the smallest intention of quitting the premises until I've spoken to Papa. And when I do leave, I shall insist upon the family coach."

To her consternation, her half brother laughed contemptuously. Inwardly seething, she leapt to her feet but restrained an impulse to slap the smirk off his sly face.

"At least you have more spirit than your lowborn mother. My father's timid, butter-wouldn't-melt-in-her-mouth mistress! The slut."

"How dare you!"

obliged to draw your cork."

"Take your hands off me, Ravistock. I'll have you know I'm in charge here."

"I beg to differ. While your father lives, he is. Furthermore, he expressly requested me to make sure you treat your sister with respect. I promised to see that you toe the line."

"The devil fly away with you, Ravistock! Always sticking your oar in where it's not wanted. What brings you here today, anyway?"

"Official business." Ravistock stared down his Roman nose at his adversary. "Since your father is bedridden, I serve as conduit between him and the Admiralty, as well you know. Do I have your word that you will refrain from mistreating your sister while she remains under your father's roof?"

"Oh, very well," the viscount agreed waspishly. "Now, unhand me."

"As you wish." Ravistock unclenched his fist.

Richmond didn't anticipate such promptness. Caught off balance, he sailed backwards into the hardwood chair directly behind with enough force to bruise an unmentionable part of his anatomy.

The likelihood brought a flicker of a smile to Diantha's face. Then, becoming aware that Ravistock had edged closer to her chair, she bravely raised her gaze, praying her inner turmoil at his nearness wasn't reflected in her eyes.

"Sebastian Pemborough, Marquess of Ravistock, at your service, Miss Fraser."

Noting her confusion, his stern face lightened with bemusement. "With your permission." He grasped her uninjured hand and raised her to her feet. "Come with me, child," he said. "I'll take you to your father."

Chapter 3

"Closer . . . come closer, child," Devonwych entreated. "These old eyes don't see well."

Diantha regarded the wizened man swaddled in satin comforters with dismay. "Sir, I am as close as may be."

The glazed stare vanished as watery blue eyes managed to focus. "Ah, there you are, my dear. So like your mama." He gave a long, shaky sigh.

"Am I truly? How I wish I had a likeness of her."

"Do you? How remiss of me." He transferred his gaze to the marquess. "Sebastian, I want Diantha to have my miniature of Maria."

"Rest easy, sir. It shall be as you wish," Ravistock assured him.

Returning his attention to his daughter, Devonwych entreated between wheezy breaths, "Your hand, child."

Diantha slipped her hand into his.

"Do you sing?"

"Yes. Not as well as Mama, though."

Devonwych gave a frail cackle. "Indeed, Maria could sing. Soprano?"

"No, my lord. I'm a contralto."

After a heavy pause, he said, "No great matter. Quality everything. Retune pianoforte. Must hear you sing."

The words had no sooner left his mouth than he was seized by a coughing spasm. Seeing his pale countenance grow relentlessly mottled, Diantha rose up from the chair the marquess had placed beside the bed for her use. She was determined to withdraw so her father might rest.

"I shall be most happy to oblige you, sir, when you are feeling more yourself."

The earl gave her hand a feeble squeeze. "Don't go. Wish to die in peace. In my grief, neglected you. Sent you away." His voice trailed, and she caught a pleading look in his watery eyes. "Forgive me, child."

Diantha couldn't bear to add to the expression of contrite misery mirrored on his deathly pale face. Drawing a deep breath, she resolutely banished the resentment she'd harboured for far too many years.

"Of course I forgive you, Papa," she assured him with quiet sincerity.

The night of the Seftons' ball found the

Marquess of Ravistock in attendance. Indeed, although the evening was still young, he'd already imprudently danced three times with the bewitching Lady Fitzwilliam, setting in motion a steady buzz of matrons whispering behind raised fans. Quite soon after committing this glaring breach of etiquette, Lord Sefton, no doubt egged on by his virtuous spouse, drew him aside to quietly register his displeasure.

"My dear Ravistock, far be it from me to censure your conduct. However, Sir Henry has just arrived, drunk as a wheelbarrow. Under the circumstances, I trust you will tone down your ardour a trifle. I dare swear my better half will never forgive either of us if her ball is ruined by an ugly scene."

As Sebastian admired his host, he was quick to beg his pardon. Their parting was amicable. Lord Sefton proceeded to mingle with his guests; Sebastian sought out his hostess to take leave of her before departing for White's.

When he arrived at the exclusive gentlemen's club, he found the comfortable establishment almost deserted. However, in the next quarter hour, his peers began to trickle onto the premises. Alvanley challenged him to a game of hazard, and feeling in need of a diversion, Sebastian accepted. An hour later, he regarded the growing stack of coins before him, pleased to see that his luck still held. Drawn by the mounting excitement, several lords had gravitated to their table, including the Earl of Jersey.

Brimming with confidence, Sebastian impulsively staked his entire winnings on the next toss of the dice. After shaking the container, he threw them onto the polished table. Then, staring down at the exposed dots, his heart sank. A collective gasp resounded in the suddenly still room. His winning streak was over.

Ravistock shrugged. No matter. He was not a dedicated gamester and had sense enough to quit before he was in too deep. He was about to make his excuses and withdraw when a wounded cry of indignation caused him to glance up. To his consternation, Sebastian found himself gazing straight into Sir Henry Fitzwilliam's unfocused eyes. In that instant, he wished he'd never heard of Honoria, wished he'd never coveted another man's wife. He suspected it was far too late for regrets. He was forced to acknowledge his luck had definitely taken a turn for the worse.

"I shay, old chap, what the devil do you mean by your overwarm attentions to my wife. The deuce take you, sir, I've a good mind to call you out."

Sebastian gave an inward sigh. "Don't waste your breath, Fitzwilliam. You're foxed. If you must demand satisfaction, approach me again when you're sober."

"But . . . ," Sir Henry floundered.

At this point, the Earl of Jersey entered the fray. With disarming affability, he slung a comforting arm round the besotted young man's shoulders. "See here, Fitzwilliam, it's bad *ton* to issue a challenge while soused. Not the thing, stripling, not the thing," he remonstrated, adding as he began to draw Sir Henry off, "besides, my cocky young buck, why work yourself up into a dander over your charming wife's latest peccadillo? I, for example, wouldn't dream of making difficulties over my spouse's romantic flings. Only think, if I ever decided to defend her honour, I'd be obliged to meet every nobleman in London. So fatiguing, don't you agree?" Lord Jersey capped his unorthodox advice with a yawn.

Perversely charmed by the nobleman's timely intervention, Ravistock almost laughed aloud.

"Excuse me."

Wheeling round, the marquess recognized the youth's livery. All trace of amusement deserted him as he drew the servant to an unoccupied corner where they might talk undisturbed.

"One of Devonwych's footmen, aren't you? Timothy, if I'm not mistaken?"

"Right, sir. 'Tis the guv'ner. Popped off while Miss were playing the piano 'e 'ad tuned."

"Pity. Devonwych was fine as they come." Sebastian fought to contain a sudden welling of moisture behind his eyes, winning the battle by a hair. "How does Miss Fraser? Is Richmond making her life miserable?"

"No, milord. Not that 'e wouldn't 'esitate if 'e be in town. 'e be at Lynchburg."

"Good!"

The footman nodded in agreement, then frowned. "Young missie took 'er father's death 'ard."

The marquess's eyes narrowed pensively. "Perhaps I can help soften the blow. Wait for me outside, Timothy. I'll join you the minute I've made my excuses."

At Cavendish Square, Higgins advised him Miss Fraser had retired for the night. Though he had no reason to doubt the servant's word, Sebastian found himself strangely reluctant to leave the premises. The silent battle of wills was broken when the butler pointedly cleared his throat.

"Would a word with the housekeeper ease your mind, milord? She took it upon herself to calm the girl down."

"It might."

"Very good. If you'll wait in the drawing room, she'll join you presently."

A few minutes later, a grey-haired woman entered. "Kind of your lordship to enquire after Miss Fraser, if I might say so."

Sebastian forced a smile. "I don't mean to be a nuisance, but I promised her father to keep an eye on her. Timothy said his death upset her."

"Indeed, it gave the lass quite a turn. Praise be, she finally drifted off to sleep."

"You were able to calm her, then?"

"Aye, milord. Happens I was her nurse when she was a wee lass, so it was easy for me to coax her into taking a few drops of laudanum."

"It appears you have the situation well in hand. Forgive the intrusion."

"To tell you the truth, sir, I'm glad to know someone of your standing has her welfare at heart."

The marquess found Higgins in the entrance hall, eager to usher him off the premises. Stepping out into the cool night air, Sebastian gazed up at the stars, a little amazed at the haste at which he'd quit White's to rush to Miss Fraser's side. True, he'd given his word to Devonwych that he'd protect the girl from her brother's wrath, but there'd been no pressing reason to beat a path to her door in the middle of the night — particularly with Richmond out of town.

In the hope of clearing his muddled state of mind, he decided to walk home and ordered John Coachman to drive on. He set off at a brisk pace, but gradually his footsteps slowed. If only Timothy had run him to ground sooner, he might have been the one to comfort Miss Fraser, instead of Crawford.

The morning of Devonwych's funeral found the marquess ensconced in the library of his town house overlooking Hanover Square. Once again he perused the letter the earl had entrusted to him. Then, tossing it aside, he strode over to the window to stare out at the falling rain.

The nerve of his mentor suggesting he wed his daughter! Bad enough the girl was illegitimate. The infamous scandal precipitated by her mother's death made the idea impossible.

His thoughts tumbled backwards. He'd been sixteen when Maria Fraser was murdered. Although they'd barely been introduced, he'd been hopelessly infatuated with her. As a consequence, he'd kept a scrapbook of newspaper clippings detailing the tragedy.

Sebastian's mouth twisted in a self-mocking grin. Unless he was very much mistaken, the scrapbook was still in his possession. He spotted it exactly where he remembered last placing it on the bookshelf. After the briefest of hesitations, he lifted it down.

The first page held a newspaper engraving of Maria Fraser standing outside the Covent Garden Opera House. On the fatal night, Lord Devonwych had accompanied his mistress to the performance but had been called away on urgent Admiralty business during the interval. Maria had been obliged to wait alone for her carriage.

No question she'd been a beautiful woman, Sebastian mused, directing his attention back to the engraving. A bleakness stole into his face as he looked at the background. The Devonwych coach with its door standing wide open was noticeable.

Maria had been about to enter when a deranged navy captain had stepped from the milling crowd, put a gun to her head, and fired. The next picture showed her crumpled upon the pavement, mortally wounded by the bullet in her temple. Her assailant had then tried to commit suicide with his other pistol, which misfired. The final engraving showed him lying in the gutter, crying, "Kill me! Kill me!" to the astonished onlookers.

The balance of the scrapbook held clippings recounting the obsessed captain's trial, conviction, and hanging. According to testimony, the murderer and his victim had never met. At first, he'd been content to worship the gifted beauty from afar, then, as his infatuation grew, he'd sent her a letter containing a marriage proposal. Maria had not responded. Feeling spurned, the captain became embittered. How dare she choose to continue to live under Lord Devonwych's protection instead of accepting his honourable offer?

Poor Maria! Ravistock sympathised. By all accounts, a chaste woman faithful to her protector, she'd been vilified by the press and by cynical members of the *ton* who'd insisted the captain must have been her lover. How else to explain his vengeful action?

Sebastian shuddered. Such a sordid affair! Certainly no one would blame him for declining to honour the earl's deathbed request. He had no objection against Miss Fraser herself, but he knew what was due his long line of illustrious ancestors.

No, of course he wouldn't marry Diantha Fraser. Not even if such a manoeuvre would serve to convince Sir Henry he no longer had any excuse to seek satisfaction. Not even if her dowry would allow him to make the necessary improvements to the country estate he'd inherited in such a run-down condition from his father.

Still, the earl had been right about one thing, Sebastian acknowledged. It *was* high time he quit playing the rake and settled down, before he became embroiled in a major scandal of his own. But first things first. He did feel honour bound to do what he could to protect Miss Fraser from her half brother. It was the least he could do, since marriage was out of the question.

It rained the day of the funeral. Timothy helped Diantha alight from the closed carriage and opened her black umbrella.

In church, listening to the rector recount

her father's achievements during the years spent at the Admiralty, she was glad she had not yielded to an unworthy impulse to punish him by withholding her pardon. How miserable she'd feel today if she'd lacked compassion when he lay on his deathbed. Instead, she felt a comforting sense of peace, in spite of the overcast April sky.

Now, as she stood at the graveside, she carefully scrutinised the faces of the noble assemblage come to pay their last respects. Did anyone recognize her after all these years? Or did she resemble Mama as much as her father had intimated?

The Marquess of Ravistock, standing on the far side of the yawning grave caught her eye and bowed. A smile touched her lips as she recalled his kindness the day he'd rescued her from Richmond.

The prayers ended. The grave was filled. Basil, without a word to her, left with his wife, a tall, gawky creature in black bombazine on his arm.

Diantha picked her way over wet, spongy grass. As she reached the carriage, Crawford left the group of servants and joined her.

As they drove, an hysterical laugh tickled Diantha's throat. As she watched the housekeeper dab at the corners of her eyes with a soggy handkerchief, her present situation struck her as ironic. She'd asked Crawford to ride in her carriage under the assumption that, should she give way to tears, her former nanny would be on hand to comfort her. Instead, here she sat dry-eyed patting Crawfy's shoulder.

After Rhoades set them down in Cavendish Square, Diantha hurried up to her room to remove her black straw bonnet, embellished for the sombre occasion with black netting. After tidying her hair, she went into the dining-room, where a cold collation of sliced ham, devilled eggs, assorted salads, and an array of pastries awaited.

Famished, she started towards the buffet, only to find her path blocked by Basil and her sister-in-law, Sophia. The latter awarded Diantha a frosty stare and said in a voice loud enough to be heard by everyone else in the room, "Miss Fraser, I suggest you retire to the scullery. I am sure you will feel more comfortable there."

As one, the other mourners gasped. Diantha felt the blood steadily drain from her head. Her first instinct was to bolt from the room. She was ready to die of mortification. Then the Marquess of Ravistock sprang to her side.

"For shame, countess," he chided. "Today of all days one would hope you might be charitable enough to keep a civil tongue in your head."

"But, milord, surely you don't expect me to break bread with my father-in-law's by-blow. It is most unseemly."

The marquess sneered. "Madam, I cannot believe you will suffer overmuch from the experience. I doubt it is the first time you have dined in the company of your betters."

Furious, Sophia turned to her husband. "Basil, are you going to let this rogue insult me?"

"Calm yourself, my dear. I'll deal with this." Richmond addressed his next remark to Ravistock. "I don't recall inviting you, Sebastian."

"I invited him, milord," confessed the family solicitor. "His presence is required during the reading of the will."

Ravistock cocked an eyebrow, amusement quirking the corners of his lips. "Of course, if you don't wish me to partake of any refreshment, I can always keep your sister company in the scullery."

"The devil take you, Ravistock. I'll have

you know I'm no nip-cheese. You are welcome to eat your fill, though why you feel it necessary to be forever defending Miss Fraser is beyond me."

"And Miss Fraser?"

"Very well. She may stay," he acquiesced.

"Your generosity overwhelms me," the marquess responded with dry sarcasm.

Before Richmond could think of a rejoinder, Ravistock presented him with a cold shoulder as he drew Diantha towards the refreshment table. "Shall I fill a plate for you, Miss Fraser, or would you prefer to make your own selections?"

"Neither, sir. In the face of the countess's insult, I cannot swallow a bite."

"Don't spout nonsense, child. You must eat."

She shook her head. "I cannot."

Ravistock frowned. "If I'd known you were going to be so contrary, I should never have rushed to your defence."

Indignation flared. "I did not ask you to defend me, my lord."

"Nonetheless, I do seem to be forever rescuing you from some scrap, don't I?" he observed, awarding her a flinty smile. "It will not do for you to cry craven. You must brazen it out. Take some food and pretend to eat if you truly cannot."

Diantha responded to his advice with a shrewd look of assessment. "Surely you realise Basil tolerates me only because he's afraid of you? You can hardly stay in my pocket forever. The instant you desert me, he'll pounce."

"Be easy, Miss Fraser. I intend to stick to your side like a burr. I suggest you fill your plate so I can fill mine. I am hungry if you are not."

With a reluctant sigh, she did as he bade. They retired with their food to a quiet alcove, where she was amazed to find her appetite had revived.

After their repast, he insisted upon escorting her into the library. Sensitive to the curious stares, Diantha was grateful when the solicitor began to read from the will, thanking her stars when it automatically diverted unwelcome attention from herself.

Shuffling feet and a subdued murmur greeted the news that Crawford, long employed by the deceased, would receive a modest annuity. Quite unbidden, hope leapt in Diantha's breast. Surely her father would leave her a little something. Even a minuscule settlement would serve as a hedge against penury, though, of course, she expected she would still be obliged to earn a living.

Her half brother, she readily acknowledged, would resent anything she might receive. A furtive glance in his direction confirmed that even the pittance awarded to Crawfy was a hard cross to bear.

Diantha could not help but be amused when she saw how Basil's spirits perked up once the solicitor touched on his inheritance. "To Basil Richmond, my son and heir to my title and the whole of my entailed properties, namely the town house in Cavendish Square and the Lynchburg estate, as well as the income derived thereof, I further bequeath the sum of thirty thousand pounds from private funds on the express stipulation that said monies be used to dower his two daughters and to provide a jointure for his wife upon his death."

The smile poised on Basil's pale countenance froze. He licked bluish lips, while glaring at the solicitor as if it were the poor man's fault. Apparently, Diantha reasoned, he resents receiving money from his sire's unentailed funds because Papa had specified how it should be spent. *Ungrateful wretch!*

The solicitor wisely avoided her brother's baleful eye as he busily shuffled the papers before him.

So much for her own expectations! Airdreams. She should never have allowed herself to presume her father would leave her any money. Though she tried not to be bitter, she could feel acid coating her throat. But she must not be ungrateful. He had educated her, and by his lights, had discharged his duty to her.

It had been his deathbed whim that had summoned her up from Kent. She couldn't help but wish he'd had the kindness to leave her buried at the ladies' seminary, rather than disrupting her life and raising false hopes.

"Finally," the solicitor resumed, "I leave the remainder of my personal fortune, estimated to be in excess of fifty thousand pounds, as well as any income derived from mining investments in Wales, to my natural daughter, Diantha Fraser, provided she agrees to wed Sebastian Pemborough, the present Marquess of Ravistock."

Diantha gasped. Her eyes sought Ravistock, lounging casually against the mantelpiece. His roguish wink put her totally out of countenance. Mercifully, after clearing his throat, the solicitor continued, and Diantha felt it would be in her best interest to pay close attention to his steady drone.

"In the event she refuses to honour my dearest wish, during her lifetime she may draw on the interest as needed, but is exempted from touching the principal. The same restrictions apply to any children born, should she choose to marry anyone else but Ravistock. Should she die without issue, my entire fortune is to be awarded to a worthy charity. Furthermore, I designate the aforementioned Ravistock as her guardian and trustee of her estate until she either marries or attains her twenty-first birthday."

At last, the droning voice ceased. A tense, uneasy silence pervaded the room. Then Sophia bounded over to Diantha's chair. "Humph! No wonder you look like the cat who got the cream! Well, you won't get away with it. My husband will contest the will."

"But, ma'am, I . . . I never dreamed . . . that is to say I . . . I had no idea . . ." Diantha drew a deep breath and stated firmly, "I did not seek this bequest."

Basil, who'd lost no time travelling to his wife's side, spoke up in a peevish tone. "So you claim. Obviously towards the end, Father went queer in the attic." He glowered at the solicitor. "How could you countenance this havey-cavey plot to rob me of my rightful inheritance? I make no doubt your palm was well greased?"

The unpresupposing solicitor stiffened in every fibre. "My lord, I strongly advise you to curb your careless tongue. Obviously, you've forgotten yourself in the heat of the moment, but if you ever dare to infer that my conduct in this affair was unscrupulous, I'll sue you for slander."

"Take a damper, Richmond," advised the marquess. "You know perfectly well your father's mind was sound. If it were not, he could never have continued to carry on his duties at the Admiralty while bedridden."

"Dash it, Ravistock, stay out of this." Basil turned to the solicitor, clumsily attempting to temper his anger. "I didn't mean to imply you were in anyone's pocket."

"All I did was follow your father's explicit orders. But for the life of me, sir, I cannot imagine why you should feel ill-used. You did inherit the bulk of his estate, did you not?"

"I did, but I had every reason to suppose I would receive the whole, and no inkling whatsoever that he meant to make an heiress out of his . . . his by-blow."

The marquess extracted a tiny snuff box with mother-of-pearl lid from his vest pocket. It sprang open at his touch. "Take care, Richmond. You are in dire danger of becoming a dead bore." He deposited a pinch of snuff in each nostril in turn, and then, as if to emphasise he would brook no further nonsense on the subject of his mentor's will, indulged in a resounding sneeze.

His indifference so incensed Basil that he trained his vehement gaze upon his half sister. "As for you, you baseborn doxie, get out of my house. This instant!"

Though still in a daze due to her unexpected windfall, her brother's ultimatum brought Diantha to her feet. Gathering the shreds of her dignity about her, she said calmly, "No need to fly into a passion, Basil. I'm already packed, so if you will dispatch a footman to secure a hack, I shall be happy to oblige."

"A footman? Such cheek! I shall instruct my servants to set your luggage on the curb. You must fetch your own cab."

Her own anger rising, Diantha made a curtsey. "As you wish, my lord." She turned away, prepared to quit the room, but her progress was checked by Ravistock.

"Miss Fraser, I cannot permit you to leave the premises unescorted."

Basil sneered. "No need to marry the wench, Ravistock. I daresay she can be moulded into a suitable lightskirt, if she's anything like her mother."

The marquess said in a dangerously clipped voice, "Apologize at once."

"Never! You're damned quick to defend her. I gather you do mean to marry her. Not that I blame you. Bastard or no, fifty thousand pounds is quite a sweetener."

Ravistock's powerful body went completely still. "You have two choices, Richmond. Apologise to both your sister and me or await a call from my second."

Chapter 4

Driving at breakneck speed, bound for Bath in his phaeton, Sebastian could only reflect that his responsibilities seemed to be growing at an alarming rate. Soon after the satisfaction of hearing Richmond's apology had come the far-from-satisfactory missive from his sister. What possibly could have sent her up in the boughs? he wondered.

A day and a night passed before he was admitted to his mother's house in Laura Place wearing travel-stained breeches and dusty topboots. Standing in the entrance hall, he heard soft footfalls on the stairs and glanced upwards.

"Sebastian! Thank goodness you've come!" exclaimed Lady Jane Bentley shortly before she threw herself into her brother's widespread arms.

Laughter rumbled from deep inside Ravistock's chest as he returned her hug. "Did you doubt it? After the heart-wrenching plea you sent?"

"Oh, I knew you wouldn't fail me. It's just that I didn't expect you quite so soon."

"I didn't spare the horses. Your note sounded too urgent."

Although Jane was thirteen years his senior, Ravistock was very fond of her. What a pity her husband had died so young, leaving her a widow with a son to raise. He set his sister back on her feet, a little apart from himself, the better to discreetly study her appearance. His dark brows came together just above the bridge of his nose. He hadn't seen Jane since Christmas, and it alarmed him that in the interim she'd lost more weight than she could afford. Clearly, she did not prosper living under their domineering mother's thumb. For even though her face boasted good bones, it had grown too thin.

In an attempt to disguise his concern, Sebastian dredged up a smile. "Excuse my dirt. You gave me no chance to make myself tidy before hurling yourself at me."

Mortified, Jane hung her head. "Forgive my want of conduct. It's just that I'm so glad you're here."

"Widgeon! No need to grovel," he reproved gently. "I was only teasing."

"Oh. Silly of me not to realise."

If only Jane had more backbone,

Sebastian lamented. After the briefest of hesitations, he fixed her with a stern look. "My dear, you do yourself no favour by allowing Mama to browbeat you."

"Yes, I know," she admitted quietly. "Trouble is, I cannot seem to change my nature."

"You could try."

She shook her head. "I lack the courage."

"What a bouncer! But tell me, what's put Mama's back up this time?"

"As usual, it's the boys."

Jane referred to their brother, Harry, a devil-may-care stripling of eighteen, and to her son, Will, who was the same age, but bookish, and thus less inclined to land in the suds.

"So I gathered. What have they been up to?"

Lady Jane sighed. "They've been sent down from Trinity College until the beginning of next term."

"Both of them?"

"I fear so."

"Good God!"

Jane's expression was glum. "The caper was Harry's idea. I did manage to pry that out of them. Yet, Will took part. More's the pity!"

"Will's as shrewd as they come. I'm surprised he followed Harry's lead."

"No more than I. I'm more disappointed than I care to say. But I didn't mean to tease you with my troubles the minute you walked through the door. I imagine you're a trifle sharp set after your journey."

At the mention of food, Ravistock's stomach rumbled. More amused than embarrassed, he responded dryly, "My dear, Jane, how clever of you to guess."

"Fustian! Wait in the library. I'll tell Digby to arrange for a tray."

"Excellent! Give me a chance to take the edge off my appetite, then send the boys to me there. Depend upon it, I'll give them the trimming they deserve."

Relief broke upon Jane's gaunt features. "Such a pleasure to have a man about the house for a change! I can't thank you enough for coming so swiftly."

The marquess arched a sceptical eyebrow. "Doing it up too brown, my dear."

Noting Sebastian's dark flush and the way he tugged at his neck-cloth as if it were too tight, Jane belatedly remembered that compliments — however sincere — discomfitted him. She found this lack of address in a man noted for his ease in Society rather endearing, and her customarily sombre features broke into a teasing smile. "Sorry, brother mine. It was not my intent to embarrass you."

"Enough idle chatter!" he admonished, then added in a softer tone, "See to the repast you promised. There's a good girl!"

"Yes, of course," Jane agreed, her facial expression once again sober. "I'll attend to it at once."

As he strode into the library, Sebastian's conscience tweaked him. Jane so seldom smiled. How thoughtless of him to dampen her lighthearted mood.

Oh, the devil! If he weren't so travel weary, no doubt he'd have exercised more patience. However, not only was he wore to the bone due to the relentless pace he'd set during his journey, but a further distraction was the muddle he'd left behind in town when he'd rushed away.

Expression rueful, hands locked behind him, Sebastian strode back and forth across the Turkey carpet. And as he paced, the sage advice, *Be careful what you wish for,* taunted him. Truth be told, after several years on the town the social whirl of the London Season had begun to pall. Worse, the lovely Honoria no longer excited him. Thus, he'd found himself seeking a new challenge. Well, he'd certainly got his wish.

Confound it, anyway!

Ravistock's expression grew pensive as he continued to ruminate. Upon Devonwych's death, he'd inherited not merely a ward, but an entirely new set of problems, all revolving around Miss Diantha Fraser. His eyebrows drew together as he wondered how she was faring in London during his absence. He'd barely had time to see her and Crawford settled in at Grillon's and to escort her on her first visit to Madame Lavelle's in North Audley Street when Jane's distracted missive had arrived. As a consequence, he'd hastily dashed off a note advising his ward he'd be out of town for several days and charging her to continue to visit the dressmaker for the scheduled fittings.

Digby's sedate entrance bearing a tray of food brought Sebastian back to the present. Firmly banishing Miss Fraser from his mind, he set down to build a mouth-watering sandwich of wafer-thin slices of boiled ham and cheddar cheese slathered with dark mustard.

A scant quarter of an hour later, the boys joined him in the library. The marquess quelled a sigh. Because his father had ever been feckless, Sebastian had long since assumed the parental role with Harry, even though he was only eight years older. Now he studied his brother intently, an element of hesitation in his gaze. While the youth deserved to have his hair combed, he didn't wish to alienate him.

"Harry, I understand you've been rusticated."

The youth's Adam's apple bobbed up and down. Nerves, Sebastian concluded, pleased that Harry was by no means indifferent to his latest fall from grace.

"Right, sir, I have."

"Care to tell me how this came about?"

"Not particularly."

"Humour me, Harry."

"Oh, very well," his brother replied, his petulant tone making his sense of ill-usage obvious. "One of the dons at Trinity took it upon himself to goad me about a tavern wench, who favoured me over him. Vowing to get my own back, I paid her a bribe and arranged for her to be found in his bed — him three parts disguised, both naked as a shorn sheep."

"You've left out the best part, Harry," Will protested.

"So I did. I neglected to mention I also sent the provost an anonymous note that caused him to come tearing into Gibby's quarters without bothering to knock." A reminiscent smile stole across Harry's features. "It was a famous setdown, Sebastian! I wish you could have been there to see the look on the provost's face."

"You did that to a don?" The marquess threw his brother an incredulous look.

The youth nodded.

Perhaps it was unwise, but for the life of him Sebastian could not resist clapping his brother on the shoulder. "I'll say this for you, Harry. You may not have been blessed with an overabundance of brains, but by God, you don't lack bottom!"

"I take that as a compliment, sir."

Like a combination punch learned at Gentlemen Jackson's Boxing Salon, a second thought followed swiftly on the heels of the first. "Good God, Harry! You don't mean Old Gibson?"

"But I do. Why? Do you know Gibby, sir?"

Snaggle-toothed, bowlegged, thin as a toothpick, the image of Gibson rose up before the marquess's eyes, obliging him to choke back a peal of laughter.

"He was a fellow when I was at Cambridge too. I'm amazed he still holds the post. I assumed he'd long since gone to his maker."

"No such luck!" Harry responded, a hint

of petulance in his voice.

Still struggling to contain his mirth, Sebastian prudently shifted his attention to his nephew, Will Bentley. "I understand you took part in Harry's scheme. What do you have to say for yourself?"

Lifting his chin to meet the marquess's gaze, Will admitted with disarming candour, "Nothing to my credit, Uncle."

Despite his determination to put up a stern front, Sebastian's lips quirked briefly at the corners. Will was definitely a chip off the old block. For not only had he inherited his father's shortsightedness, making spectacles a necessity, he'd also fallen heir to his scholarly bent and lack of guile.

"I can understand how Harry got entangled. He can never resist a lark, but I thought you had more sense, Will."

"Old Gibson deserved to be taken down a peg. He had no business tormenting Harry."

The boys had a point. Sebastian found it impossible to deny it. Still, he could hardly allow them to get away with what they'd done. "That may very well be true, but . . ."

Harry interrupted. "It's not Will's fault, sir. Someone gave him a glass of blue ruin, and being a trifle bosky, he went along with my plan without a murmur."

Will peered through his spectacles at the marquess, his demeanour rueful. "I never had so much as a taste of the vile brew before, sir. I know it's no excuse, but it did warp my judgement."

"So I gather. Look here, you two, I know Old Gibson is a loose screw, but you're getting too old to cut up larks. You especially, Harry."

"I know it. But somehow I can't seem to stop."

"In my opinion, what you need is a lengthy dose of rusticating with ample time to consider how best to mend your ways. Therefore, I order you both to remove to Teale House and strongly suggest, while rusticating, you give some serious thought to becoming less irresponsible in future."

"What? Banished to the wilds of Wiltshire!" Harry gave a derisive snort. "Dash it all, Sebastian! It's deuced flat there this time of year."

"I am not sending you there to enjoy Society. A health slice of solitude is just what you need to come about. Besides, in another month or so, the streams that cut into Teale Manor will be teeming with fat trout, just begging for you to throw in a line."

"But, Sebastian . . ."

"No buts, Harry," Ravistock countered, a hint of steel in his tone. "I'll see you on your way bright and early tomorrow morning. Is that clear, boys?"

The marquess's gaze swept from one youth to the other, his expression stern and unyielding. Will nodded first; Harry took longer to capitulate and did so with ill grace.

After dismissing the boys, Sebastian sauntered over to the double French doors that led out to a small walled garden. Staring out at the leafless trees, he decided Harry was right. Though mid-April, the grounds looked dismal. No wonder the lad had balked at being banished to the country.

Ravistock frowned. Perhaps it had been a mistake to insist Harry attend Cambridge instead of buying him a commission. But the marchioness wouldn't hear of it. Harry was her favourite. She'd flown into a rare pucker. No son of hers was going to end up cannon fodder!

Sebastian had elected to break the impasse with a counterproposal. He'd insisted Harry attend Trinity College for at least one year, after which time, should he still have his heart set on becoming an officer, Sebastian would buy him his colours. But in retrospect, in view of the fact that his brother was no scholar, perhaps it had been an unwise decision.

At least Jane should be pleased with today's outcome, he reflected. Much as he abhorred being obliged to pose as the authority figure, he felt he'd acquitted himself well. He was now free to return to London and plunge himself back into the social whirl.

Sebastian's eyebrows came together in a frown. No, he couldn't. Miss Fraser awaited his return to town. Thanks be to God he needn't marry her if he didn't wish to. And he didn't. Truth be told, he didn't wish to marry anyone at present. After all, he was only six and twenty, and while he'd been on the town ever since he'd left Cambridge with a first, it had only been recently that the fair sex had become so eager to bestow their favours.

Sebastian's mouth twisted in a cynical smirk. Honoria wouldn't have spared him a passing glance six months ago. Doubtless his assumption of his father's title was responsible for his sudden popularity. But, despite his disillusionment, he wasn't quite ready to settle down.

The door opened, and his mother deigned to make a grand entrance. The Marchioness of Ravistock was built on solid lines with a square-shaped torso, buttressed by a bosom that could only be described as imposing. To round out the picture, her ladyship's countenance bore an unfortunate resemblance to that of a disgruntled bulldog. In addition, she possessed a booming voice that most people found decidedly unsettling.

Needless to say, beauty was not what had prompted Sebastian's sire to pay his addresses. What had enticed him as a young man to come up to scratch was the fact that her ladyship's father had been a nabob willing to settle a fortune upon his dowd of a daughter on her wedding day.

"Sebastian, you rogue!" The marchioness wagged an accusing finger at her eldest son. "How could you be so unfeeling as to skulk about under my roof for the better part of an hour without informing me of your arrival?"

Ravistock flinched as her voice set the Sevres porcelain cup and saucer to rattling on the tray. Nonetheless, despite his mother's lack of beauty and her bluff mannerisms, a wave of affection broke over him as he studied her features. God knew there were prettier, more feminine-looking women, but despite her blustery bossiness, he'd always known she was fond of him and wished him well.

"I ask you, is that any way to treat the woman who brought you into the world?" she chided, her short sturdy arms akimbo.

"Pray forgive me, Mama. Jane was in such a state I thought it best to call the boys to book first."

"Very pretty speech, my dear. But what it boils down to is that I've been relegated to the last place on your list." Her eyes snapped with indignation.

"Now, Mama, don't you dare fly into a taking. I've been two nights on the road, and I'm in no mood to soothe wounded sensibilities."

Ill humour forgotten, the marchioness gave a good-natured cackle. "That's what I admire about you, son. You're never afraid to stand up to me. Come give me a kiss."

As he neared, Sebastian winced inwardly at the sight of his mother's gnarled fingers, swollen at the joints. The poor dear had arthritis and was often wracked with pain. No wonder her tongue was so tart on occasion. His lips brushed his mother's raddled cheek.

"I might have known that ninnyhammer daughter of mine would waste no time summoning you."

"Mama, I wish you would not call Jane names. She deserves more respect."

"Fiddle! What a piece of work you are making of a slip of the tongue."

"Be fair, mother. You know you bully her."

The marchioness looked momentarily chagrined. "I'll grant you, Jane has many sterling qualities, but she's such a mouse. If I say 'boo,' she jumps. I can't seem to resist the temptation."

"Shame on you, Mama! For Jane's sake, I hope you will mend your ways. Promise me you'll try."

"Oh, very well, I give you my word," she agreed sulkily. "But enough on that head. Called the boys on the carpet, did you? Trust you settled their hash."

"I banished them to Teale Manor until the fall term."

"It will be hard on those two rapscallions to be buried in the country, but I daresay it won't hurt them."

"My sentiments exactly." Sebastian sent his mother a disarming smile. "Not to change the subject, but since I have your ear, I wonder if you'd do me a favour?"

The marchioness's grating laugh rang in his ears. "Depends on the favour. I'll have you know I've cut my eye teeth."

"Fair enough, Mama. Are you aware the Earl of Devonwych died recently?"

"Certainly. We get all the London papers here in Bath. I read his death notice. I'm sorry for your sake. I know you were close friends. I venture to say you'll miss him."

"That I will — despite the fact that he made me guardian of his daughter."

"Daughter? You must be joking. To the best of my recollection, he didn't have a daughter."

"His natural daughter, Mama."

"Merciful heavens! Are you referring to the child Maria Fraser bore him?"

"I am. Devonwych left the girl a fortune. I'm to manage it until she either comes of age or marries."

"Well, if that don't beat all! Friend or no, you're a nodcock to have agreed."

"There was no one else he could turn to, Mama."

"That comes as no surprise. Who else would be so foolish?" the marchioness scoffed. "Mark my words, in view of the scandal, no one will marry the chit."

"Yes, they will. She's an heiress."

"How very odd of Devonwych to leave

76

her his money! But then, he was always eccentric. Most noblemen set their mistresses up in separate quarters and visit them there. They don't make a practice of living with them *en famille* in a fashionable Mayfair town house!"

"I willingly concede Devonwych was a trifle odd, but he was my friend and mentor, Mama. That is why when he asked me to look after Diantha, I felt I could not refuse."

The marchioness sighed. "As a boy, you always had a soft spot in your heart for strays and waifs. I'd thought you'd outgrown it. No such luck!"

"To move directly to the crux of my problem," Sebastian paused to draw a fortifying breath, then hurried on before he lost his nerve, "she cannot live at Hotel Grillon indefinitely, so I was wondering if I could persuade you to let her stay with you here in Bath, until we find someone to marry her."

"What? Bring the infamous Maria Fraser's offspring to live under my roof? Have you taken leave of your senses?" Indignation reigned undisputed upon the marchioness's homely features. "I've a good mind to box your ears! How dare you even suggest such a course? The answer is no!

Don't think you can twist me round your finger like you usually do! I guarantee you won't."

"Mama, do calm down. There's no need to fly into the boughs. If you won't put her up, you won't. I promise I won't tease you any further. The subject is closed."

"Humph! I sincerely trust so. Now, I believe I'll retire to my room and lie down. For the first time in a donkey's age, I feel positively fatigued."

Chapter 5

Ravistock jumped down from the box of his high-perch phaeton and handed the reins to his tiger with a smile.

"I shan't be long, Jeremy. Mind you don't keep the horses standing."

"Don't you worrit, guv'ner. Trust me to look after 'em proper," stated the under-sized lad with fervour.

Thus reassured, Ravistock entered Grillon's with a spring in his step. He took no notice of the plush crimson carpet underfoot or of the gold-embossed ceiling. He was too busy giving himself a pat on the back. After all, hadn't he handled Harry and Will's latest misadventure with cool despatch? Surely, if he put his mind to it, he'd be equally successful in sorting out Miss Fraser's affairs as well.

"Hurrumph!"

The pointed clearing of a male throat close by interrupted his thoughts. Fixing his gaze upon the obsequious hotel clerk,

Sebastian cocked his head to one side and enquired, "You wished to speak to me?"

"Indeed, my lord, I truly hate to trouble you, but Grillon's has got rules and regulations."

"I expect you do," the marquess acknowledged coolly. "Have I inadvertently broken one?"

The clerk flushed. "I hope I know my place better than to presume to accuse your lordship of any such infraction. I was speaking of your ward."

Good Lord! What had the chit been up to during his absence? "Oh? What's she done?" he asked.

The clerk shuffled his feet as if uncomfortable under Ravistock's steady gaze. "The young lady's taken in a common alley cat. Your Lordship must understand that while we value your patronage, the sorry creature's not fit to pass through this establishment's portals."

"How disobliging of Miss Fraser, to be sure. Did you advise her of her infraction?"

"That I did, my lord. Got nowhere for my pains. So I decided to appeal to your honour, as you're the young lady's guardian."

"How very astute of you! I assure you I'll take the matter up with her."

"Excellent!" The clerk hesitated, then, obviously unwilling to let such a golden opportunity slip through his fingers, plunged on. "Don't mean to press, but if my lord could see to its removal today, I'd be most grateful."

Ravistock blinked at this latest piece of effrontery. "My dear fellow, I don't work miracles," he advised. "You must be patient. Miss Fraser's father died recently. I don't wish to overset her."

"Your scruples do you credit, my lord. Still, rules is rules."

The marquess indulged in a discreet yawn. The lowly minion was fast becoming a nuisance. Sebastian favoured him with a look that boded ill for his health, should he be so foolish as to detain a peer of the realm much longer.

"I'll bear that homily in mind. Now, if you'll excuse me . . . ?"

"Certainly, my lord." Bowing and scraping, he stepped out of the way.

Freed from the constraints of civility, the marquess didn't spare the clerk another thought as he strode across the lobby and up the stairs. Indeed, his mind was still busy trying to decide how best to persuade his ward to give up the cat she'd so unwisely befriended when he rapped on the door of her suite.

Diantha poured milk into a saucer. When she set it on the floor, a scrawny, half-grown kitten bounded across the carpet. In its eagerness, it almost tumbled headfirst into the shallow dish, but somehow managed to skid to a halt in time to avoid disaster. After consuming every drop, it trained beseeching eyes upon its benefactress.

"Want more, do you?" Her eyes brimmed with sympathy. "Poor little lad, here you go."

She emptied the rest of the pitcher's contents into the saucer. Once again the undernourished kitten's pink tongue set to work. Like an anxious nanny, Diantha hovered nearby. Fortunately for her peace of mind, by the time it had licked the saucer clean a second time, its tummy was so full, it staggered a little as it walked.

Diantha grinned. "Well done, Caesar! Continue to lap up your milk like that and you'll soon be fat!"

The kitten blinked, then calmly proceeded to lick its paw.

"Look, Crawfy!" Diantha cried. "He's grooming himself. Isn't he cunning?"

Crawford glanced up from the merino

shawl she was knitting for her sister. "Fustian! All cats do so."

"Really, Crawfy, must you be such a wet goose?"

"Mind your tongue, miss!"

"Yes, ma'am. I'm sorry."

"Don't think to turn me up sweet. I can just imagine what your guardian will have to say about all the fuss you've caused."

Diantha glared at her companion. "I might have known you'd side with him. All Ravistock has to do is smile and you're ready to dance to his tune."

Crawford's ruddy complexion reddened even more as she said stiffly, "What did you expect me to do when his lordship asked me to accompany you to this hotel? Let you come here without a chaperone?"

"Oh, Crawfy, I sound like such an ingrate!" Diantha exclaimed, overcome with remorse. "I know how much you were looking forward to retiring to Sussex with your sister. Naturally, I'm grateful you agreed to postpone your plans so you might lend me countenance. But, don't you see, I couldn't let Caesar starve without lifting a finger?"

"I suppose not. Too bad your charity has landed you in management's bad books."

"Oh, pooh!" Diantha scoffed. "Who

cares a fig what they think?"

"More fool you if you don't!" Crawford yanked upon the ball of yarn resting at her feet. "Mark my words, miss! Should they take a notion to toss us out on our ears, you'll soon change your tune."

While Crawford delivered her scold, Caesar awoke and intrigued by the unraveling strand of yarn, rushed to investigate. Unhappily, before either woman divined his intent, the rambunctious kitten had managed to become entangled.

"Now see what he's done," the housekeeper wailed. "Taking him in was a mistake! That skein cost the earth!"

Diantha cradled the kitten in her arms. "Pray strive for a little calm, Crawford," she recommended. "I'll soon set things right."

True to her word, with sure, deft fingers Diantha managed to separate the struggling cat from the ball of merino in record time. Unhappily, the instant Caesar was free of his bonds, he bolted across the room and proceeded to claw his way up to the top of a panel of silk brocade flanking a tall window.

Crawford wrung her hands. "That naughty kitten! Bad enough he tangled my wool. Now he's bound and determined to

84

rip the draperies to tatters! Best get rid of him before he turns the place into a shambles."

"How can you be so heartless! He's only a kitten. He'll learn."

Diantha was engaged in coaxing Caesar to loosen his hold on the silk brocade, when the firm rap on the hall door caused her to give a startled jump.

Crawford frowned. "Mercy, who can that be? Not one of the staff, I hope! They're sure to cut up stiff if they get wind of our mischief maker's latest trick!"

A second knock prompted Diantha to ask with a faint trace of acerbity, "Are you going to answer it, or shall I?"

"I'll go. You see to the kitten."

As Diantha stepped upon the straight chair and reached for Caesar, she heard Crawfy exclaim, "Lord Ravistock! How fortunate. I feared you might be one of the staff."

Sebastian laughed. "I take it they've been pestering you about my ward's cat."

"That they have, my lord. Plaguey lot!"

"I brought my carriage. I thought Miss Fraser might enjoy a drive through Hyde Park this afternoon."

"Lovely! Come in, my lord. You can wait in the sitting room while Miss Di changes."

At the sound of their approaching footsteps, Diantha gave an alarmed squeak. Her hand strained to reach the emaciated kitten clutching the silk brocade, desperate to retrieve Caesar before the marquess entered. Failing, Diantha stood on tiptoe.

"Mercy! Have a care what you're about, miss!"

"Don't shout at me, Crawfy!" Diantha remonstrated as she plucked the cowering cat off the drapery.

Unhappily, her sudden motion threw her own weight off balance. Beneath her feet, the chair teetered ominously, but fortunately she had the presence of mind to leap to the carpet shortly before it toppled backward.

"What did I tell you, Crawfy! Didn't I say I'd get him down in one piece?" Diantha crowed.

"You . . . you little idiot! You could have hurt yourself!" barked the marquess.

With the trembling ball of fur nestled protectively against her breast, Diantha whirled round to face him. "So you're back."

Sebastian's strong, sensitive mouth twisted in a sardonic smile. "None too soon it seems. I see you've acquired a pet."

Diantha eyed him suspiciously. "If you've come to persuade me to give

Caesar up, save your breath."

"Miss Di! Mind your manners!" the housekeeper admonished.

"Yes, ma'am." Momentarily subdued, Diantha settled into a comfortable arm chair and began to stroke the kitten curled in her lap. Caesar began to purr.

"You appear smitten with that scruffy creature," Sebastian observed gruffly. "But then, there's something appealing about a purring cat."

"I quite agree." She beamed fondly at the dozing kitten. "Caesar appears to have worn himself out with his latest misadventure."

"Just so."

Diantha threw Sebastian an apologetic look. "I fear my manners have gone abegging. Pray be seated, my lord."

"Thank you, but the purpose of my call is to invite you for a drive."

"Famous! May Caesar accompany us? Do say yes. He needs an outing as much as I do."

Diantha could tell by her guardian's expression that allowing her kitten to go along was the very last thing he desired. Thus, she was overjoyed when he gave a resigned sigh and said, "Very well. Bring him if you must."

"Splendid!"

Diantha excused herself to change. A scant twenty minutes later she reappeared attired in a stylish carriage dress of grey bombazine. She carried a wicker basket.

The marquess rose to his feet. "That was quick."

Diantha gave a rueful grin. "I was taught not to dawdle at the seminary."

"New bonnet?"

Her lips curved as she pictured it in her mind's eye. Composed of grey *velours simule*, lined with white sarcenet, edged with black gauze ruching, it was definitely top of the trees.

"Yes. Do you like it?"

"Very fetching."

She dipped him a saucy curtsey. "Thank you, my lord."

"I take it Caesar is inside the basket? Do you want me to carry it?"

"No, my lord, I can manage."

The marquess gave a laconic shrug. "As you wish. Come take my arm," he commanded, his look defying her to refuse.

Instead, with a sweet smile, she slipped her arm through his and let him lead her from the suite.

The instant Diantha spotted the high-perch phaeton waiting at the curb, her heart beat faster. Painted dark green with gold trim, sporting bright yellow wheels, its high-gloss surface gleamed in the sunlight.

"Gracious, is that your carriage?"

Sebastian awarded her an indulgent smile. "Yes."

"The boy holding the horses' heads. His livery matches your phaeton."

"Stands to reason. Green and gold are traditional family colours. Jeremy's my tiger."

"Tiger?"

"A homeless brat who has wormed his way into my affections."

"Like Caesar did to me?"

The marquess chuckled. "Precisely. Jeremy accompanies me whenever I choose to drive my phaeton. Dressed in his finery, he joins me on the box, supposedly adding to my consequence. Of course, when I invite a lady for a drive, she shares my seat and he rides on the platform in back."

After a brief silence, Diantha observed with brash sincerity, "My lord, Jeremy's almost as scrawny as Caesar. I think you should speak to your cook."

Much struck by her ingenuous remark, Sebastian laughed. "So he is. Perhaps I shall."

Diantha eyed the driver's seat. "The box is very high off the ground. I doubt I can climb up there hobbled by my skirts."

"You disappoint me, Miss Fraser. Naturally, I assumed anyone so intrepid as to risk their pretty neck in order to rescue a recalcitrant kitten — who'd just made mincemeat of an expensive window hanging — possessed sufficient courage to at least make an attempt."

Outflanked, Diantha decided her best defence was the truth. "Much as I hate to play the coward, the perch is just too high."

"Even if I give you a boost? Trust me, Miss Fraser. I won't let you fall."

Strangely enough, she did trust him. Besides, she'd been looking forward to the outing and was reluctant to forego the anticipated pleasure. Thus resolved to brush aside her fears, she managed to say with only a faint quaver, "Very well, Lord Ravistock, I place myself in your hands."

The trust shining in her eyes evoked a rush of tender feeling within Sebastian's breast. Shaken by unexpected emotion, he adopted a brusque tone. "Set the basket on the sidewalk so I may lift you onto the box. Once you are seated, I'll hand Caesar up to you."

Before Diantha could protest, he'd relieved her of her burden and hoisted her aloft. When he lifted the basket, she silently prayed the lid wouldn't fly open, allowing Caesar to escape. When her fervent plea to the heavens carried, she set the basket on the seat beside her — where she could keep an eye on it. Only then did she feel free to sink back against the gold tabaret upholstery.

Soon after, the precariously balanced phaeton swayed and rocked as Ravistock climbed aboard and Jeremy scrambled up behind. The marquess glanced at the wicker basket on the seat between them before raising his gaze to scan Diantha's face.

"Ready, Miss Fraser?"

"Yes, my lord." As ready as she'd ever be, considering her misgivings, she silently amended.

"Then we're off." At his deft flick of the reins, the chestnuts sprang forward.

By the time the phaeton turned onto Park Lane, Diantha was thoroughly enjoying the exhilarating sensation of bowling along at such a smart clip. Studying the marquess's strong, capable hands as they expertly managed the ribbons, she tried to understand what it was about the man that made her feel safe whenever circumstances threw them together. As if she were confident he'd protect her from harm.

She was being silly. After all, he'd been gone from town a sennight and she'd managed to survive. Still she had not expected to miss him, but the truth was London had seemed flat without him.

Sebastian cleared his throat. "Miss Fraser, I visited Madame Lavelle's shop on my way to your hotel. When I arranged for you to have a complete wardrobe designed by one of the top mantua-makers, I had no idea of offending. You see, knowing the vast majority of your sex would be in the alts at such a prospect, I naturally assumed you'd be equally pleased."

Diantha felt her cheeks grow hot as she recalled how she'd fidgeted while being fitted. "I am not so bird-witted that I despise beautifully made clothing."

"I stand corrected," he teased. "I assumed it was the tedium of all the necessary fittings to which you object."

"Quite right! An entire week devoted to nothing else is enough to overset the most placid of females. Moreover, I see no need for so many gowns. After all, I am in mourning."

"True, but though your situation restricts activities such as dancing, many other diversions are considered unexceptional. Now that your wardrobe is complete, I mean to see that you get about a bit more."

Diantha sent him a searching look. "Pardon my curiosity, but what sort of diversions are considered appropriate, in light of my background?"

Ravistock's jaw dropped. But to his credit, he made a swift recovery. "Since you appear to admire candour, may I be equally frank?"

"Nothing could please me more."

"Splendid! Despite your er . . . somewhat irregular background, with the exception of your half brother and sister-in-law, I believe a great many congenial members of the *ton* will receive you. You are, after all, an heiress."

Diantha bristled. "In other words, the money my father settled upon me mitigates the stigma of my birth."

"My dear Miss Fraser, Society is not so gothic as Richmond intimated. Happily, in addition to your large dowry, on your father's side at least, your lineage is impeccable."

"Poor Mama! It hardly seems fair to lay the entire blame for my predicament at her door."

"What a diverting, if inaccurate, notion! While undeniably true that Maria evolved from yeoman stock, her beauty and musical gifts may be considered points in her favour. The problem, of course, is that your parents could not marry. Regrettably, your father was already wed, albeit unhappily. But as I was attempting to explain before we got off on this tangent, there are a number of activities that a young lady in black gloves may indulge in without risking censure. Daily carriage rides in the park, sightseeing, ice's at Gunter's, small dinner parties, the opera . . ."

"The opera, my lord?" she asked with quickened interest.

Sebastian chuckled. "I collect, in common with your beautiful mother, you're a lover of music?"

"Indeed I am."

"I see. Perhaps you would care to accompany me to the opera some evening?"

Diantha regarded him with shining eyes. "What a splendid notion!"

He laughed. "I'll arrange it then. Now since we've reached Hyde Park Corner, I suggest you observe the cream of the *haut ton* engaged in their daily promenade."

Chapter 6

No sooner had Ravistock slowed the horses than he exclaimed, "Devil a bit!"

Diantha looked askance. "What's amiss?"

"Curse our luck! Lady Jersey is signalling me. It won't do to offend her. Nothing for it but to acquiesce to the forthcoming inquisition gracefully."

"Inquisition, my lord?"

"Without a doubt. A word of caution, Miss Fraser. Let me do most of the talking. I'm an old hand at eluding Sally's verbal snares."

"Very well, my lord."

The instant the marquess drew up alongside Lady Jersey's carriage, Diantha was captivated by the beautiful matron's striking raven hair and perfect complexion.

"Queen Sarah," as Sally Jersey was dubbed by her peers, greeted Sebastian with a cool smile. "You're a deep one, Ravistock. I gather the young woman beside you is Lord Devonwych's daughter."

"It is. Allow me to do the honours."

Once introduced, the countess fixed Diantha with a basilisk stare. "So what do you think of the *ton*, Miss Fraser?"

Diantha was taken aback by her ladyship's forthright query. "Indeed, my lady, I have no opinion."

Lady Jersey raised a sceptical eyebrow. "Come, come, miss!" she chided. "It is useless to try to fob me off with your die-away airs!"

"I shouldn't dream of being so uncivil," Diantha assured her earnestly. "You see, this is my first drive in the park."

Her ladyship appeared much struck by Diantha's artless revelation. "My compliments, Ravistock. I find your ward's directness rather taking."

Sebastian smiled sweetly. "No doubt you do. It appears to be a trait you have in common."

The countess looked stunned by his comment, but after a moment's reflection, chuckled good-naturedly. "A pox on you, Ravistock! You seem to know my failings all too well."

"Just so, my lady."

With a faint glint of malice in her piercing gaze, Sally Jersey observed with deceptive blandness, "Perhaps you would be good enough to tell me when the banns are to be posted?"

Instantaneously, all levity vanished from the marquess's demeanour. "Despite Miss Fraser's undeniable charms, I have no plans to marry at present. Now, I must beg you to excuse us. I don't like to keep my cattle standing too long."

Seconds after they'd resumed their promenade, Diantha plucked at Ravistock's sleeve and, once she had his attention, admitted with a rueful smile, "You were right to caution me to guard my tongue. Lady Jersey is rather intimidating."

"Oh, Sally's not so bad. Pity she's so fond of gossip."

As the phaeton continued its leisurely ramble along Rotten Row, Diantha, unsure of how to broach a topic that was cutting up her peace, swallowed, then darted her guardian a speaking glance. "I cannot think where she got the notion we plan to marry."

"Certainly not from me!" Ravistock snapped.

Diantha sat a little straighter on the box. "Nor from me, my lord," she affirmed stoutly. "Still, it is obvious someone spoke out of turn, else Lady Jersey wouldn't know of my father's skipbrained notion that we wed. Moreover, since I am not the party who tattled, I wish you'd cease to glare at me in that odiously superior fashion."

Sebastian threw back his head and laughed. "Little termagant! You are quite within your rights to call me to order. Pray excuse my abominable manners."

"Certainly, my lord."

No doubt Richmond, or possibly his wife, had been spreading tales. No one else knew the terms of Devonwych's will. Sebastian gave an inward sigh. His duty was clear. Somehow or other, he must convince Richmond it was not in his best interest to bandy his half sister's name about.

"Gracious!" Diantha exclaimed.

Thoughts interrupted, Sebastian sent her a quizzical look.

"Who's that gentleman in brown?" she asked.

Ravistock redirected his gaze towards a handsome Corinthian clad in brown from head to foot and driving a brown carriage pulled by horses of the same colour.

"That's Petersham."

"Since you know him, perhaps you can explain why . . ."

"Do hush. He's almost within earshot," Ravistock warned in a gruff undertone as he pulled the chestnuts to a halt.

Petersham greeted the marquess with a nod. "Haven't seen you in your usual haunts of late, Ravistock. Still interested in that snuffbox you admired?"

"Most definitely. Been out of town. Had to make a flying trip to Bath to bring Harry to book."

"You have my sympathy. A younger brother must be the very devil to watch."

"It's not so bad. Just curst inconvenient."

"Quite. Dare I ask how you found the marchioness?"

Sebastian acknowledged the hit with a bark of laughter. "Too bad of you to roast me, Charles. Mama's as contentious as ever. Anything interesting happen while I was away?"

Petersham smirked. "If you will pardon the pun, a battle royal appears to be in the offing. King's dug in his toes. Refuses to listen to his minister's advice. Claims only a divorce will satisfy him. As to the queen consort, rumour has it she's arrived in France and is only waiting for the most propitious moment to cross the Channel."

Sebastian shrugged. "I daresay it will be

all sorted out in the near future, since Prinny will be anxious to put the coronation ceremonies behind him."

"No doubt you are right. But we're being impolite. Kindly introduce me to your lovely companion."

"Certainly. My ward, Miss Fraser. Diantha, this is Lord Petersham."

Diantha awarded him a winsome smile. "Forgive me, Lord Petersham, but I cannot resist the impulse to ask you if there is any significance to your er . . . brown study?"

"Diantha!" Sebastian reproved.

She slanted him a mischievous look. "Did I say something amiss?"

Before he could respond, he was distracted by Petersham's shout of laughter. Ravistock waited with growing impatience for the nobleman to recover his composure. At last, Petersham wiped tears of mirth from his eyes. Then, riveting his gaze upon Diantha, he saluted her with his brown beaver hat.

"My dear, you are an original. But to answer your question, I was once infatuated with a widow named Brown. When she spurned my addresses, I adopted this monochromatic form of dress. Though my affections are no longer engaged, I see no reason to widen my spectrum."

Diantha giggled. "Judging by the sour expression on my guardian's face, I collect I should not have quizzed you."

"Don't tease yourself. I find your candour refreshing."

Petersham's obvious delight in Miss Fraser's pert directness did not sit well with the marquess, who viewed this unexpected turn of events with a jaundiced eye. Even though his purpose in making his ward known to Society was to encourage eligible suitors — thus getting her married and off his hands — somehow or other, the spirited exchange between Diantha and Petersham rankled.

Forcing a smile, Ravistock proceeded to lie through his teeth, "Charles, I'm delighted you're so taken with this saucy minx, but I fear we are holding up traffic."

As if emerging from a daze, Petersham glanced about them. "So we are. Miss Fraser, dare I hope to see you at the Castlereagh rout this evening?"

"I fear not, my lord. I am in mourning."

"Miss Fraser's comeout is postponed due to her father's death," Ravistock was pleased to explain.

"Pity that. Adieu, Miss Fraser," Petersham said, tugging on the reins.

The marquess set his horses in motion, and once they'd moved out of range, asked, "What do you think of Petersham?"

"Handsome, well-mannered, charming," Diantha admitted.

Ravistock frowned. "He's a confirmed bachelor on the wrong side of forty. Much too old for you."

Diantha treated the marquess to a searching look. "My lord, I have not set my cap for him. I merely found him diverting."

"You relieve my mind." Sebastian gave a dry chuckle. "While Petersham has many admirable qualities, he's a Stanhope. Eccentricity runs in the family. In my opinion, his preference for a single colour to the exclusion of all others is an odd quirk, the charms of the Widow Brown notwithstanding."

"How cynical you are. I prefer to think he still secretly pines for his lost love."

The marquess eyed her with unabashed speculation. "I collect you are a romantic. I, myself, am a pragmatist."

"I detest being pigeonholed. So demeaning."

"Yes, but practical," he quipped.

"You are teasing me. Too bad of you, my lord!"

She turned to glare at him, but when she glimpsed the laughter in his eyes, her indignation melted and her mouth curved.

Returning her smile with interest, Sebastian observed sagely, "All this my lording grows tedious. While, for propriety's sake, it behooves us to use surnames when addressing each other in public, do you object to my calling you Diantha when we are private?"

"No, my lord," she replied demurely.

"Good. My Christian name is Sebastian," he informed her pointedly before resolutely transferring his gaze to the high-stepping chestnuts in harness.

Sebastian. A name the tongue could savour, she decided. Who would have imagined a drive in the park during the fashionable hour would prove so diverting?

Without warning, Sebastian's lopsided grin faded under the stress of feathering a corner to avoid a collision with a curricle approaching from the opposite direction. The delicately balanced phaeton tilted dangerously. While Sebastian struggled to quiet the nervous horses, Diantha clutched the seat with both hands to prevent herself from sliding off the box.

Then, to her dismay, the wicker basket

toppled off the seat to the floorboards. On impact, the lid flew open. Caesar leapt into her lap, then sprang to the marquess's chest, where he dug his claws into his lordship's satin waistcoat.

Reflexively, Ravistock cuffed the spitting kitten. Losing purchase, Caesar fell between the traces.

"The horses! He'll be trampled!"

Terror clogged Diantha's throat as she scrambled down from her high perch. The instant her feet hit the ground, she scooped the cowering kitten out of the path of the phaeton's spinning wheels.

"Diantha!" Sebastian thundered.

He yanked on the bridle with desperate strength, tossed the reins to Jeremy, and vaulted to the ground. There, he pulled Diantha close to his pounding heart.

Seconds later, anger superceded fear. "Of all the henwitted, addlebrained starts, yours takes the palm!"

He plucked the cat from her startled grasp, picked the basket up off the floorboards, and plopped the culprit inside. Slamming the lid shut, he handed it up to Jeremy. "Stow the demmed basket in a safe place if you value your hide."

Determined not to quail in the face of adversity, Diantha gamely met Sebastian's irate glare. "How dare you browbeat me after my close scrape?"

"You're lucky I don't wring your neck. Scared the hell out of me!"

"Sebastian! Such language!" she reproved him.

His grin was sheepish, but the expression in his eyes was shrewd. "Minx! Never mind my language, you should never have taken such a risk."

"Indeed, I'm sorry I distressed you, but I had to rescue Caesar."

Ravistock stared at her. Beyond a doubt, she was the most exasperating female who'd ever crossed his path. Yet, while he deplored her impulsiveness, he had to admire her courage.

He shook his head as if to clear it, the gravity of his countenance belied by the twinkle in his eye. "Troublesome baggage! Whatever am I going to do with you?"

Diantha lowered her lashes shyly. "I . . . I daresay I try your patience."

"You do manage to keep me on tenterhooks," he confessed with an ironic smile.

Her cheeks flushed a delicate rose. Now that the danger was over, Sebastian had an overwhelming urge to run his knuckles lightly across her soft skin. When he'd seen her standing a mere hairsbreadth away from the bucking horses, raw fear had squeezed like a vise about his heart. Never had he felt so powerless. The possibility that she might have been trampled had been agonising.

Emerging from his daze, the marquess ordered Jeremy to climb down and stand at the horses' heads, then turned to Diantha. "We are obstructing the free flow of traffic. Permit me to lift you onto the box so we may get under way."

She tossed him a tentative smile. "As you wish."

His heartbeat picked up the instant he slipped his hands around her slender waist. As he raised her aloft, he silently acknowledged that more and more often he felt himself in danger of succumbing to the intoxicating lure of her innocence. Fortunately, he had a strong sense of honour. As Diantha's guardian, it would be unconscionable to take advantage. Thus, though reluctant to end the intimate contact, he released her promptly.

He'd just joined her on the box when he heard his name called and redirected his gaze. "Good Lord! Honoria!" Ravistock swore under his breath.

Though Diantha didn't catch the mumbled words, she sensed her guardian was vexed. She glanced first at his grim profile and then at the approaching carriage.

"Oh," she gasped, suddenly self-consciously aware of her dishevelled appearance, for the open landau contained the most beautiful woman she'd ever seen.

"Sebastian, my love, is it really you?" queried the enchantress.

Her tinkling laugh made Diantha's heart ache. Was the beauty's relationship with Ravistock as close as that laugh intimated?

"Good afternoon, Lady Fitzwilliam."

He gave a cautioning nod towards Diantha. Her ladyship blithely chose to ignore his hint. "Bother doing the civil!" she scoffed, her green eyes aglint with speculation. "What sort of rig are you running?"

"Don't be absurd. All I'm up to is an afternoon drive."

"So you claim. But something's afoot. Why else would you turn up at the fashionable hour looking as if you've taken a tumble in a dustheap?"

The question was unanswerable. The marquess decided to ignore it. He gave a deep sigh. "Lady Fitzwilliam, allow me to introduce you to my ward, Miss Fraser."

The nasty glint in Honoria's eyes as she looked Diantha up and down caused the latter to give an involuntary shiver.

"So this is the heiress born on the wrong side of the blanket." Honoria glared at the marquess. "How dare you foist this . . . this ragamuffin upon me, sir? *I do not care to make her acquaintance!*"

Concluding her tirade with a disdainful sniff, Lady Fitzwilliam huffily ordered her coachman to drive on.

Grim-faced, Ravistock watched the landau merge into a crush of slow-moving carriages. Then, girding himself to face an overset female, he darted an anxious glance at Diantha. What he saw made his lips twitch. Her bonnet hung rakishly askew. Several raven ringlets had escaped a once-neat coiffure to dangle enticingly at her temples. Sebastian dug into his pocket and offered her his handkerchief.

"Here," he said. "You look as though you could use this."

Diantha brushed it aside with an angry swipe. "I don't need it. It will take more than her ladyship's snide tongue to reduce me to tears."

Her outburst prompted him to take a closer look. While true she wasn't yet crying, she was on the verge. Touched by her determination not to lose her composure, he said bracingly, "Of course you will not cry. I absolutely forbid it!"

Diantha stared at him intently. But instead of the mockery she expected to find, the expression in his sherry-coloured eyes warmed her through and through.

"There's a smudge on your cheek," he explained. "If you will allow me."

When she voiced no objection, he raised the handkerchief to her face and gently wiped it clean.

A disturbing sense of intimacy lingered long after he'd returned the crumpled square of linen to his pocket. Mildly troubled by this unexpected turn of affairs, Sebastian was almost glad when he espied a tuft of cat fur on his coat sleeve. With a moue of distaste, he plucked it off.

Diantha struggled to contain a bubble of laughter. "Oh, dear," she said in a strained voice. "I do believe one of your silver buttons is missing."

Sebastian darted a glance at his coat. Not only was he missing a button, but thanks to that curst kitten's claws, his satin waistcoat was snagged beyond redemption. As for the mathematical arrangement of his neck-cloth, he nursed a strong suspicion it no longer enjoyed the same degree of perfection that it had when he'd set out on his afternoon ramble.

After a moment's contemplation, the

humourous aspect of their situation occurred to him and the corners of his mouth quirked. "Disgraceful! My valet will be appalled."

Diantha responded with a shaky laugh. "Nor will Crawfy be best pleased with my appearance."

His eyes skimmed her ruined satin slippers, lingered upon a laddered silk stocking, revealing a tantalising glimpse of trim ankle, before resolutely moving on to the torn flounce of her carriage dress.

The marquess gave a rueful chuckle. "By God, we're a sorry-looking pair."

Diantha giggled. "So we are, sir! So we are!"

Chapter 7

On the way to the Castlereaghs' that evening, Ravistock took advantage of the fact that he was alone to let loose a string of oaths that would have done justice to the crustiest old salt that had ever been impressed into His Majesty's service.

Obviously, introducing a cat of Caesar's ilk into his household at Hanover Square had clearly been ill-advised. Shortly after he'd handed over the ingrate to a footman with orders to convey the wiggly wretch to the kitchen, pandemonium had ensued below-stairs.

The marquess had been involved in the delicate process of arranging his neck-cloth when Parker, his high-in-the-instep butler, had seen fit to override the protests of his valet and invade his dressing-room.

"Tonight's dinner will be cold mutton," Parker advised.

Sebastian raised an eyebrow. "Oh? I expected roast beef."

"Cat's to blame, milord. Darted in front of the kitchen maid. Tripped, she did, and dropped the platter. The cook had a fit."

Now, as the carriage bowled along successive Mayfair streets, the marquess pinched the bridge of his nose. If he had any sense, he'd have turned the wretched kitten off to fend for itself the minute his phaeton passed out of sight of Grillon's. But how could he? In order to persuade Miss Fraser to entrust him with her kitten, he'd promised it would receive the best of care under his roof. Honour demanded he keep his word.

All the world and his wife appeared bound to attend the Castlereagh rout, Sebastian mused as he descended from his coach in front of a torch-lit mansion. Certainly Honoria wouldn't dream of missing such a gala affair. No time like the present to call her to account for cutting his ward in Hyde Park. Jaw set in a firm line, he vowed not to waste a moment seeking her out.

Once inside the ballroom, he scanned the crowd. No sign of Honoria. Initial frustration gave way to amusement when he espied his handsome host dancing with his plump wife. When the set ended, the devoted couple came arm-in-arm to greet him. Straightening from his bow over the viscountess's hand, Sebastian said, "You are very light on your feet, ma'am."

Castlereagh beamed at the compliment. "Isn't she just. Emily's naturally graceful. In Vienna, she mastered the German Waltz almost immediately, whereas I was reduced to dancing with a chair before I learned the step."

A vision of the British foreign secretary twirling his wooden partner was too tempting to resist. Sebastian gave a crack of laughter. Castlereagh favoured him with an amiable smile that indicated he took no offence.

Emily lightly tapped her husband's knuckles with her fan. "What fustian! The Congress of Vienna was ages ago. You've been waltzing creditably for years."

"My dear, you flatter me."

Good manners dictated that Sebastian solicit a dance from his hostess. However, before he could overcome his reluctance to put a period to the Castlereaghs' light-hearted banter, Honoria joined them.

Bold as brass, she tucked her arm in his. "What delayed you, Sebastian? I'd almost given you up."

Her possessive gesture stirred his resentment.

Honoria accorded the Castlereaghs a brittle smile. "I need to speak to Lord Ravistock. Is there a room close by where we may be private?"

Castlereagh looked taken aback. "By Jove, I really don't think . . ."

Honoria batted her eyelashes coquettishly. "Do give over, my lord," she entreated their host. "The matter is urgent."

Castlereagh tugged at his neck-cloth. He looked ill at ease, yet determined not to budge. At this point, his better half took pity and intervened.

"Relax, my dear," Emily advised, affording Honoria a cool glance. "I believe the small salon at the end of the corridor adequate to your purpose."

"Thank you, my lady." Facial expression smug, Honoria gave the marquess's arm an imperious tug. "Do excuse us."

Inwardly seething, Sebastian managed to hold his tongue until they'd entered the parlour. Then freeing his arm from her viselike grip, he shut the door and leaned back against it.

Obviously vexed by his lack of ardour, Honoria flounced across the room and seated herself on a boldly striped sofa. "Pray do not indulge in a fit of the pouts, Sebastian."

Ravistock gritted his teeth. She was lucky he'd confined his displeasure to sulking. What he'd like to do is tear a stripe off her hide for being so rude to Diantha at Hyde Park. Yet he dare not risk it. Honoria was spoilt. At the barest hint of a scold, she'd be sure to set up a howl guaranteed to draw the gossipmongers. So instead of chastising her for her want of conduct, he contented himself with the supercilious lift of an eyebrow.

"Surely this confrontation could have awaited a more propitious moment."

Immediately below the daring décolletage of her gown, Honoria's generous bosom heaved with indignation. "Fie on you, sir! I should have been happy to behave more discreetly, had you not made a point of avoiding me the past sennight. No doubt you've been too busy courting Devonwych's by-blow to spare me a thought."

The marquess awarded her a calculating look. So jealousy had motivated her insolent behaviour.

"My dear, you are mistaken. I have not been dancing attendance upon Miss Fraser this past week. I've been in Bath sorting out a family matter."

After thinking it over for a minute,

Honoria sent him a tremulous smile. "What a ninny I am to have doubted you!"

"Don't tease yourself. I ought to have sent round a note."

"So you should have!" she agreed. "What else was I to think with the tattlebaskets insisting you planned to marry the chit." Honoria peeked at him through her lashes. "You're not hanging out for an heiress then?"

Sebastian shook his head. Evidently Diantha's half brother had been very busy spreading malicious rumours amongst the *ton* depicting himself as a fortune hunter.

"Miss Fraser is my ward, not my intended."

Honoria brightened perceptibly. "I might have known you are too wily to enter into a misalliance. I assume you and I go on as before?"

Sebastian drew a long breath. Honoria had just given him a perfect opening to make a clean break. Of course, it took a brave man to face her ladyship in a temper. But, although he wasn't feeling especially courageous, he doubted she would dare throw a tantrum in the middle of a ball. All things considered, Sebastian decided he couldn't afford to pass up this chance to give Honoria her *congé*.

"I don't wish to mislead you," he cautioned. "I intend to give serious thought to setting up my nursery in the near future."

Her ladyship responded with a shrill laugh. "Of course you must do your duty. But I see no reason for you to do without your *cher amie* — unless of course you contemplate a love match."

Sebastian tugged on his starched neckcloth that suddenly seemed too tight. Clearly, his intention of letting Honoria down gently was foundering on the shoals of her ladyship's obstinacy. Regrettably he must speak more plainly. "My matrimonial intentions aside, I wish to sever our connection."

"What?" Lady Fitzwilliam's eyebrows shot ceilingward. "After all we've meant to each other? Surely you jest."

"On the contrary, madam, I'm quite serious. You sealed your own fate when you snubbed my ward this afternoon in Hyde Park. Very uncharitable of you, my lady. Now, I suggest we end our *tête-à-tête* before we become the latest *on-dit?*"

Much later the same evening, inside the book-lined study of the marquess's town house, the fire on the grate burned low. Sebastian stretched his arms taut to relieve cramped muscles. Ought to have been in bed long since, he conceded. Yet he couldn't relax; couldn't sleep. Not too surprising since Sir Henry had dogged his footsteps all evening.

Sebastian gave a mirthless chuckle as he stared into the dying embers. He'd begun to jump at shadows — with good reason. He kept running into Fitzwilliam far too often for it to be mere coincidence. For instance, tonight their paths had crossed twice. Once at the Castlereaghs', then later at Brooks's.

The marquess grimaced. The mere thought of his close call at the Castlereaghs made his blood run cold. Had Honoria's jealous spouse arrived a scant fifteen minutes earlier, he might have discovered Sebastian closeted with his wife!

Ravistock's eyes narrowed pensively. He may have ended his affair with Honoria, but Sir Henry continued to be a problem. The fact that he'd bumped into Fitzwilliam again — this time at Brooks's was decidedly odd. Particularly, since he preferred White's, but had deliberately shunned that establishment — solely to avoid running into Sir Henry twice in one evening. Thank God he'd made a clean break with Honoria. Hopefully, once Sir Henry learned of this, he'd quit following

Sebastian around like a jug-bitten moonling.

The marquess strode purposely from the room. It was very late. High time he sought the arms of Morpheus.

Seated in the Marquess of Ravistock's private box, Diantha's stomach fluttered with nervous excitement. Bedazzled by the Royal Opera House's vermilion walls generously trimmed in gold, she was tempted to pinch herself. Above the steady hum of low-keyed conversation, her ears picked out the discordant sounds of instruments tuning up for the performance. Then the houselights dimmed, the audience quieted, and the orchestra launched in the opening bars of Mozart's *The Magic Flute*. Diantha closed her eyes, the better to allow the music to work its charm.

Indeed, she became so caught up in the score that she was barely aware the first-act curtain had fallen until Sebastian touched her arm and, in response to her questioning look, said, "Intermission. Care for a stroll?"

She gazed up at him, dreamy-eyed. "Wh . . . what?"

The marquess awarded her an indulgent grin. Unlike most ladies of quality, who visited the opera to preen and be admired, Diantha had totally immersed herself in the musical score.

"Fancy a short stroll and a glass of lemonade?"

"Splendid idea!" Eyes sparkling, she turned to her companion. "Shall we fetch you a glass, Crawfy?"

After Crawford declined the offer, Sebastian took Diantha's elbow and guided her from the box. The corridor was jammed with operagoers. Young bucks, resplendent in black evening dress, escorted high-born ladies richly bedecked with family jewels. Diantha and Sebastian managed to take only a few steps before Petersham waylaid them.

"Good evening, Miss Fraser."

"Lord Petersham. I collect you are a music lover."

Eyes dancing, he shook his head. "Much as I hate to disillusion you, I don't care a fig for opera."

"You puzzle me, sir. If that's how you feel, why attend?"

"Outspoken as ever, I'll be bound." He gave an appreciative chuckle. "Isn't it obvious? I come to see and to be seen."

A bit later, sipping lemonade, Diantha weighed her disillusionment with Petersham. Since he did not share her passion for music, he'd make her an unsuitable husband. For nothing could be worse than to wake up some morning wed to a man indifferent to music.

As Sebastian escorted her back to their box, Diantha stifled a self-mocking laugh. What colossal conceit! She'd only spoken to Petersham twice. Yet she already regarded him as a suitor. Peagoose that she was!

Once again the music swelled. For a second time that night, Diantha came under the spell of the opera. Indeed, even when the curtain fell, signalling the second interval, her sense of bliss lingered. Then Richmond invaded the box. Like a dash of ice water thrown in her face, his sudden appearance wrenched Diantha from her musical trance.

A self-righteous expression on his pale countenance, the present Earl of Devonwych glared at the marquess. "Sir, your conduct as guardian to an innocent miss leaves something to be desired. How dare you treat my sister like a common lightskirt? How dare you bring her here without a chaperone?"

Diantha felt every muscle in her body tauten. There was no love lost between them. Basil's interest in her welfare could only be feigned. Just what was his game?

"Take a damper, Richmond," Sebastian advised coldly. "I wouldn't dream of compromising your sister. Mrs. Crawford accompanied us here — as is proper."

Peering into the dim recesses of the box, Basil spotted his father's housekeeper plying her knitting needles. "Devil take you, Ravistock!" he blustered. "If Crawford's here to preserve the proprieties, why hide her in the shadows?"

"Not your concern. Appears to me you owe me yet another apology."

Sensitive to the harsh, unrelenting note in the marquess's voice, Diantha glanced from one man to the other. The day of her father's funeral, Richmond had insulted them both. Sebastian had forced him to back down. She could only pray her brother had sense enough to do so on this occasion as well.

"Don't see why I need to apologize for an honest mistake," Basil whined.

"Nonetheless, you will. I insist upon it," Sebastian responded, the unmistakable hint of steel in his voice.

"Very well, I beg pardon."

"Not very gracious, but I accept. Next time, get your facts straight before you voice any wild accusations."

Sebastian's gaze had already begun to slide away from Richmond's face when a glimmer of malicious triumph in Basil's pupils gave him pause. He's up to something, the marquess sensed intuitively. His eyes flew to Diantha. His gaze softened, and a surge of fierce protectiveness permeated every fibre of his being. By heaven, if Richmond thought he'd let him harm a single hair on her head, he was very much mistaken!

Sebastian's train of thought was interrupted by Lady Jersey's personal page's entrance into their box bearing a note. After a quick scan of the contents, he transferred his gaze back to Richmond for several tension-filled heartbeats. Was he was being overly suspicious? Sebastian gave an inward sigh. This was neither the time nor the place to decide what Richmond's real motives were. That being the case, he seized upon Lady Jersey's invitation to visit her box as an excuse to take leave of Diantha's mealymouthed brother.

Just before they stepped inside Lady Jersey's box, Sebastian squeezed Diantha's hand and, when she gazed at him quizzically, urged quietly, "Chin up, my dear. Sally won't eat you. Give you my word."

Diantha forced a smile. "No doubt you are right. Basil's impromptu visit overset me."

"Pointless to dwell on it," advised the marquess. "Ready to beard the lioness in her box?"

She shrugged. "Why not?"

They entered Lady Jersey's box. Diantha's attention was drawn to a mature beauty whose gaiety seemed spontaneous as she chatted with Sally Jersey. Shamelessly eavesdropping, Diantha overheard her say, "My dear Sally, though I am quite determined she is my last child, I regard my newest daughter as a treasure."

"Have you named her yet, Em?"

The unknown beauty wrinkled her nose. "I cannot decide. Anything but Caroline. It is a name disgraced."

"Well, of course, my dear," Lady Jersey commiserated. "Considering the trials you've had to bear, your attitude is perfectly understandable."

Diantha could not help but be intrigued. To her mind, Caroline was a perfectly lovely name. Thus, when the lady resumed talking, she was careful to keep an ear perked.

"Fanny I like pretty well, and also Mary," mused the beauty. "I've written to my brother, Freddie, in Frankfurt requesting his opinion."

"Very wise. Em, I've a confession to make. I lured you here to discuss a possible voucher."

"Not tonight, please! I refuse to ruin a pleasurable evening." The noblewoman's hands flew to her temples. "People are as mad as ever about Almack's and plague me with their applications."

"My dear Emily, there is no need to fly into a fidget. The young lady I have in mind doesn't require a voucher this spring."

"That's a relief!" Emily exclaimed.

"I beg your pardon, ladies. Do we interrupt?" the marquess enquired.

Lady Jersey awarded him a feline smile. "No, indeed, Ravistock I see you have Miss Fraser in tow. Permit me to present her to Countess Cowper."

Diantha dipped a curtsey. "My lady, I am honoured to make your acquaintance."

Kindhearted to a fault, Emily Cowper set about putting her at ease. "What is your Christian name, child?"

"Diantha, my lady."

"Very pretty. Perhaps I should add it to my list. Unless, of course, you object."

"Not in the least," she assured her ladyship, then on impulse blurted, "If you please, ma'am, I'm dying of curiosity. Why do you consider Caroline a name disgraced?"

Flustered, Lady Cowper twisted her wedding ring round and round on her finger. "Dear me. Did I say that?"

Diantha pressed her fingertips to her lips, wishing she could recall her question.

Sebastian patted the agitated Countess's hand in a consoling manner. "Please excuse my ward's impertinence, my lady."

Diantha raised her chin. While she regretted her rash outburst, she would have preferred to make amends herself.

"Pray don't tease yourself," Emily Cowper begged the marquess. "I am persuaded she did not mean to be rude."

Lady Jersey chimed in. "Em's right, Ravistock. Personally, I find Miss Fraser's inability to dissemble charming. Pity she's in mourning, else I'd be tempted to send her a voucher this spring rather than next."

Sebastian gave a sardonic chuckle. "Be warned. I shall hold you to your pledge next season."

Lady Jersey looked momentarily floored, but gamely rallied. "Indeed, Almack's has grown entirely too stodgy of late. I daresay it would be vastly amusing to allow Miss

Fraser to cross its portals."

"Just so, Countess," Ravistock responded, his sombre demeanour belied by the twinkle in his eye.

The warning bell sounded.

"We'd best resume our seats," said Sebastian.

"Needs must when the devil drives," Sally Jersey observed gaily.

Sebastian whisked Diantha along the corridor so fast that she arrived back at their box breathless. As they entered, Crawford glanced up from her knitting to frown her disapproval of their tardiness. Indeed, they'd barely taken their seats when the music resumed.

At the conclusion of the evening's performance, Sebastian suggested they linger until the crowd thinned. Still in Mozart's thrall, Diantha agreed.

"I don't wish to nag," he stated quietly. "However, you must learn to think before you speak. You embarrassed Lady Cowper."

Diantha lowered her gaze. She felt terrible. "I know I did." She began to play with the fringe edging her shawl. "I'm . . . sorry."

Ravistock took due note of her bowed head and relented. "Fortunately, Em's too

127

good-natured to take offence. But do be more cautious in future."

"I will," she promised, then knit her brow. "Curiously enough, I still don't understand why my question overset her."

The marquess grimaced. "It is no secret Prinny detests his wife, Caroline of Brunswick. Wants to divorce her. Surely you are aware of the Bill of Pains and Penalties he insisted be introduced in the House of Lords."

"Yes, of course. However, for all we know the queen consort may be proved innocent of the charges. In any case, it doesn't explain why my ill-timed query distressed Lady Cowper."

Ravistock sighed "Quite simple, really. Emily's sister-in-law is Caro Lamb. Need I say more?"

"Caroline Lamb?" Diantha's grey eyes widened. "The hoyden so smitten with Byron she pursued him dressed as a page?"

"The very same!"

"No wonder my question put her ladyship out! Will I ever learn to curb my tongue?"

Rising, Sebastian said lightly, "Enough said on that subject. Time we got under way."

He led Diantha from the box into the

now all-but-deserted corridor. At the foot of the stairs, he glanced at Diantha. "I trust you enjoyed the music."

"It was delightful. Especially the singers. I adore singing myself, you see."

Sebastian raised an eyebrow. "My dear child, I trust you aren't comparing your voice with that of a trained professional."

Spirits dashed by the censure in his tone, Diantha responded with quiet sincerity, "Indeed, I hope I'm not that conceited."

"You relieve my mind," Sebastian drawled, resolutely ignoring the flash of pain he saw in her eyes. "Frankly, amateurish female caterwauling sets my teeth on edge." After an uncomfortable lull, he added, "I trust I've not offended you with my bluntness."

"Not at all," she lied, prudently filing his confessed aversion for future reference. "But I am forgetting my manners. Thank you for inviting me. It's been an age since I've had such a treat."

"Not since your mother's death, I collect?"

"Quite! Am I so transparent?"

"Only to me . . . I would hope."

Diantha shot him a quizzical look, her breath catching in her throat at the tender regard in his gaze.

Since neither of them seemed anxious to tamper with the fragile web that ensnared them, who knows how long they would have stood gazing into each other's eyes had not Crawford's terse snort of impatience shattered the mood.

Just as well, Diantha decided crossly. What had gotten into her, anyway? She'd been staring at the marquess like a lovesick widgeon.

The patter of light footfalls captured her attention. Curiosity primed, Diantha glanced in the direction of the sound and gave a gasp of surprise.

Lady Fitzwilliam sprinted across the marble floor of the vast foyer. "Save me! Save me!" she cried as she rushed pell-mell into Ravistock's arms.

"Honoria, what's amiss?" he asked with genuine concern.

"Henry's in hot pursuit. He's in a frightful temper."

"Damnation!" All but certain she'd deliberately staged the confrontation, Sebastian's initial sympathy gave way to pique. "Here he comes. Get hold of yourself, madam."

Ravistock tried to disengage himself, but since Honoria clung to him like a limpet, his attempt came to naught.

"Unhand her, you blackguard!" cried the incenced Sir Henry as he caught up to them.

"I would gladly oblige you, sir," Sebastian responded with alacrity. "Unfortunately, it seems your lady wife has fainted."

Chapter 8

Diantha's gaze flitted from Sir Henry to Sebastian to Honoria. A niggling suspicion took hold. Thanks to a year spent teaching wilful young misses, she was well aware of their fondness for melodramatic poses. Lady Fitzwilliam might have a few more years in her dish, but Diantha suspected she was cast in the same mould. Convinced Honoria was feigning unconsciousness, she leaned over, enquired solicitously, "Are you all right?" and slyly pinched her.

Lady Fitzwilliam started. Her green eyes flashed. Sebastian looked astonished, then cynical. Diantha hid an irrepressible smile behind her hand. Imagine someone as astute as Ravistock being taken in by such an obvious ploy. Men were such innocents!

Sir Henry glowered at Sebastian. "By Jove, this time I won't be fobbed off," he crowed. "I've caught you red-handed! I demand satisfaction."

Fitzwilliam would be well served if he

accepted his challenge, Sebastian reflected. However, the deceitful strumpet in his arms was not worth risking either man's neck. With a grim smile, he thrust Honoria straight into her astounded husband's arms.

"What the devil?" grumbled Sir Henry.

"You misread the situation, sir! Your wife fainted. That is all."

"So you claim. Dashed if I see why I should take your word for it."

Sir Henry's disgruntled expression called to mind a pugnacious bully spoiling for a fight, Diantha decided. Uncomfortable with the mounting tension, she shot Sebastian a shrewd glance. Oh dear. Judging by the grim set of his jaw and his clenched first, he was prepared to defend his honour.

She fought a surge of rising panic. Sebastian could be hurt . . . even killed. There must be no duel! Diantha awarded Fitzwilliam a commiserating smile and said with sweet sincerity, "Sir, what you imply is preposterous. Sebastian has no use for a mistress. He's engaged to me."

Sir Henry's jaw dropped. "Ravistock, is this true?"

The marquess appeared equally stunned. Although his recovery was swift, there was a gleam in his eye that Diantha found vaguely disturbing.

"You heard the lady. Miss Fraser is about to make me the happiest of men."

Honoria gasped and slumped into a genuine faint. Staggered by the leaden weight in his arms, Sir Henry's air of cocky belligerence melted away.

Sebastian's gaze drifted from the unconscious Honoria to Sir Henry. "She'll be more comfortable resting on the couch against the wall. Need any help?"

"Thank you, no," Fitzwilliam responded stiffly.

Made uneasy by Sir Henry's unsteady gait as he wove toward his destination, Sebastian followed close on his heels. And since his arm now encircled Diantha's waist, she had no choice but to keep pace. While Fitzwilliam arranged his wife's inert form upon the French Empire sofa, Sebastian turned to Crawford, who hovered nearby.

"Do you carry smelling salts?"

"That I do. Step back, sirs, I beg you. If I may be so bold, what her ladyship needs is room to breathe."

"I suggest we do as Crawford says, Fitzwilliam."

Sir Henry looked determined not to

budge. But a glance at his wife's pale countenance melted his resistance.

While Crawford waved a vial under Honoria's nose, Sebastian awarded Sir Henry a placating smile. "I am persuaded that even you — suspicious chap that you are — cannot believe I'm so lost to propriety that I'd set up a flirtation with your lovely spouse in the presence of my fiancee."

Fitzwilliam glowered at him for several tension-charged seconds before distrust gave way to common sense. "Blast! Seems I've made a cake of myself. I had no idea your affections were engaged."

"Don't refine on it," Sebastian recommended.

As Honoria began to rally, Diantha cast her guardian a wary glance. The look of unholy glee that danced in the depths of his amber eyes unsettled her. What he must think of her brazen conduct! Deeply embarrassed she lowered her lashes.

In her bedazed state, Diantha was only marginally aware of being ushered from the opera house and assisted into a closed carriage.

"Crawford, you look worn to a thread," the marquess observed once he'd escorted both women to their hotel suite. "I suggest you retire and give Miss Fraser and I a chance for a brief *tête-à-tête*."

The housekeeper looked hesitant. "I'm not sure it would be proper, sir."

"Pray don't be nonsensical. Miss Fraser and I need to discuss our betrothal, don't we, my dear?"

"Y— yes," Diantha whispered.

Crawford threw up her hands. "So be it!"

The instant they were alone, Sebastian said, "My dear, whatever possessed you to tell such a whisker?"

"I . . . I know it was very bad of me, but Sir Henry was so very angry. I was afraid if I didn't step in you'd accept his challenge."

"You lied to protect me?"

"Y— yes."

Sebastian regarded her steadily, a curious light in his gaze that made it impossible for Diantha to look away.

"Do you know, I cannot remember the last time someone looked out for me — usually it's the other way round. But, my dear, although I'm flattered beyond words, your intervention was quite unnecessary. I'd have fobbed him off. You see, I abominate duels."

Diantha tossed him a puzzled look. "If that's how you feel, whatever were you about when you challenged my brother at my father's funeral?"

Sebastian responded with a mirthless chuckle. "A calculated risk. Richmond's a coward. I knew he'd back down."

"What if he hadn't?"

Sebastian shrugged. "I'd have met him of course. I simply prefer to settle my differences in a more civilised manner, whenever possible."

"Very commendable." Diantha was quiet for a minute, then asked, "Whatever will we do if the Fitzwilliams noise about my Bambury tale?"

"Then the fat's in the fire!" he admitted. "Unless I send an announcement to the *Evening Post*, the *ton* will soon realise it's all a hum."

"I'm truly sorry to have caused so much trouble."

"Not at all," Sebastian assured her kindly. "At least you bought some time."

"Time, my lord?"

Sebastian nodded. "Time for Fitzwilliam to cool off. Time for it to sink into Honoria's thick skull that I won't be swayed by her machinations."

"I see." Her expression thoughtful, she seated herself and motioned him to a chair. "Lady Fitzwilliam's so beautiful. No wonder you couldn't resist her."

Diantha's ingenuous remark brought a twinkle to the marquess's eyes. "You are not precisely in the common way yourself," he teased.

Her complexion flushed a delicate rose. "Oh? Does that mean you think I'm pretty?"

"Very," Sebastian admitted gruffly. A muscle in his cheek twitched as he resisted an almost overwhelming urge to gather Diantha into his arms. Sternly, he reminded himself he hadn't yet broached the subject of primary importance. "I know the hour is late, but please hear me out."

Fighting a yawn, her response was a tad acerbic. "I will — unless of course I fall to sleep first."

"Tact will never be your long suit," he observed dryly. "But, to get to the point, I confess I've been giving your father's wish that we wed serious thought."

Diantha's eyes held a stricken look. "You disappoint me, sir! I would never have pegged you as a fortune hunter."

"Don't be ridiculous," he scoffed. "I'm comfortably fixed."

She looked confused. "If you are not hanging out for an heiress, perhaps you would be good enough to explain precisely why you suddenly think we should marry?"

Of all the cow-handed proposals he took the palm! Sebastian mentally castigated himself. It was only natural Diantha would be suspicious of his motives. Moreover, if he broke down and confessed he loved her, she'd never believe it. To be honest, he found it hard to believe himself. The sensation was too new. One minute, she'd been his ward, someone he'd grown to like and respect — at most a treasured friend. But tonight at the same instant she'd leapt to his rescue, he'd tumbled into love.

Diantha glanced surreptitiously at Sebastian. The last thing she wanted was a marriage of convenience. She loved him too much to settle for that. She gazed at the handkerchief she was twisting. Never would she forget the instant she'd laid eyes on him. At the time she'd thought what she felt was a schoolgirl crush that would soon fade. But, her love for him had not waned. If anything, it had grown stronger. No, considering the depth of her feelings, an arranged marriage would be intolerable.

Sebastian could not fault Diantha for being wary. By rights, she ought to have a proper comeout. But, for all he knew she'd fall head over heels in love with some unscrupulous rake on the lookout for an heiress. Sebastian clenched his jaw. He couldn't take the chance of losing her. They must marry at once. It was the only way he knew to keep her safe.

Safe? The word echoed and re-echoed in his ears. Good Lord! How could he have forgotten the inherent menace in Richmond's malevolent gaze at Covent Garden?

"If we marry I can protect you."

"Protect me? From whom?"

"Richmond, of course. I'm convinced he'll stop at nothing to get his hands on your fortune."

Diantha shivered. "So that's what prompted tonight's false show of concern!"

Sebastian experienced a pang of regret. What a pity he couldn't have left her in blissful ignorance. However, Richmond was no longer content to skulk about behind their backs casting aspersions on his sister's character. No, unless Sebastian's intuition played him false, Richmond had embarked on a more ambitious scheme.

"I suspect your half brother intends to try and wrest your guardianship from me!"

"B— but my father appointed you. Surely the courts won't allow it."

"We cannot be entirely certain. Should Richmond bring suit, there are factors that could cause a judge to rule in his favor."

"Whatever do you mean?" she asked, increasingly round-eyed.

"The scant seven-year difference between us is unfortunate, whereas, if I were in my dotage, no one would lift an eyebrow." His mouth twisted in a cynical smile. "In addition, you and Richmond are blood relations, whereas I most definitely am not."

A wild look — that of a caged bird — crept into Diantha's eyes. "I won't live under Basil's thumb. I'd rather drown myself in the Serpentine."

"Too drastic by far. Marry me instead?"

"Must you keep harping on that string? Be serious."

"I am being serious," he affirmed quietly.

"My lord, a man of your consequence should look higher for his marchioness."

"I don't care a tinker's damn for my consequence."

Unnerved by his fervent outburst, Diantha nibbled the inside of her lower lip. "Well you ought to. Setting aside my, er . . . irregular background, becoming a marchioness strikes terror in my heart. Don't you see, I should not have the least idea how to go on?"

Careful not to startle, Sebastian edged closer. He brushed her cheek with his fingers, his touch feather-light. "My dear, you shimmer and shine like a newly minted penny. Protocol can be learned. I will be patient."

The subtle odour of musk intermingled with his manly scent drew Diantha like moth to flame. Troubled by vague yearnings she didn't understand, she babbled, "I've other flaws as well. At the seminary, the pranks I played often tried the headmistress's patience. Worse, there's my irrepressible tongue. At present you find it amusing, but once the novelty wears off, my outspokenness is bound to embarrass you."

Once again he brushed her soft cheek. "Better an outspoken wife than a devious jade. Marry me, Diantha."

Her eyes stung with unshed tears as she struggled to retain her composure. "Only consider, as my guardian, you're merely stuck with me until I marry or reach my majority. Should I accept your offer, it is a lifetime sentence."

"Fustian! Have I ever complained about my duties as guardian?"

"No, but —"

"I swear I've your best interests at heart.

Say you'll marry me, Diantha."

Lord only knew she was tempted. His liquid velvet baritone voice played havoc with her heartstrings. If he loved her, she wouldn't hesitate. But of course he did not. On the other hand, she silently argued, maybe she was being inexcusably stubborn. Maybe she ought to lay her childhood dream of a love match to rest. Who knew — maybe as time passed — he might come to love her.

"Say yes," he repeated softly.

His touch warmed her blood. A sweet, searing ache gradually permeated her body. What was the use of continuing to refuse him? Sebastian wasn't about to give up. He'd keep on whittling away at her defenses until she agreed to marry him.

"Very well, my lord," she said in a voice husky with emotion. "I'll marry you — if you are certain that's what you want?"

"Splendid!"

Dipping his head, he saluted her soft, pliant mouth with a brief, but tender, kiss. Her breath smelt as sweet as a newborn babe's. He was tempted to kiss her again, but she was such an innocent, he decided he'd best proceed slowly so as not to alarm her. Pulling a few inches away, his chest swelled as he noted the wondrous expression in her eloquent grey eyes.

"Time you were abed, sweetling!"

"But —"

"No buts, my love. I'll pay you a morning call. We can discuss the details of our wedding arrangements then."

The matter settled to his satisfaction, Sebastian took leave of his newly betrothed. But later, ensconced in his study sipping a drop of brandy to help him unwind, he suffered a sharp twinge of conscience. Was it wrong to pressure Diantha to wed him? Instantly, he recalled the malice he'd seen in Richmond's eyes. No, by God, he was doing the right thing!

Once Diantha was his wife, he'd be able to shield her from her half brother's sly importuning. Moreover, it would be far easier to persuade the *ton* to overlook her illegitimacy — not to mention the notorious scandal involving her mother. Indeed, as his marchioness, Diantha would be acceptable to the highest stickler. But best of all, the taking minx would be his to protect and cherish.

As the coach and four entered Hanover Square, only the slight tremour in Diantha's cheek hinted at her inner agitation. Today she was to be married to the

Marquess of Ravistock by special license.

The closed carriage drew to a halt. Diantha peered out the window, too preoccupied to admire St. George's handsome high-pillared colonnade. A footman in green and gold livery let down the steps and helped her alight.

Once she had both feet on the ground, Viscount Petersham greeted her, his expression frankly admiring. "My dear Miss Fraser, you look lovely."

Diantha's complexion pinkened. "You flatter me, sir."

"No such thing," he assured her. "Truth is I envy Ravistock. Clever chap stole the march on all the rest of us eligibles."

"Gammon!" She shot him a look of amused disbelief. "Were you waiting for me?"

"Yes. I've the honour of escorting you to the altar and giving you away at the propitious moment. So come along quietly, my dear, and none of your sauce!"

Diantha gave a peal of laughter. Petersham grinned and asked gruffly, "Feeling more the thing?"

"I . . . yes. Thank you, my lord."

"Do call me Charles. And now, my girl, while your courage is up, shall we march down the aisle?"

Smiling, she slipped her hand through the crook of his arm. "By all means."

At the altar, a wave of panic assailed her when Petersham let go of her arm in order to take his place beside the groom. The vicar began to speak. Diantha's stomach knotted. Then, Sebastian gave her hand a gentle squeeze. His caring gesture reassured her she wasn't making a horrible mistake. Pulling herself together, she struggled to give the clergyman her full attention. However, his colorless drone seemed to come from a great distance. Try as she would, she could not dispel a sense of unreality. It was as if she were a mere spectator viewing the nuptials from afar.

"Diantha?"

The tender exasperation in Sebastian's low-voiced murmur wrenched Diantha from her bemused state of mind. Botheration! Both vicar and bridegroom were staring at her expectantly.

Looking as if he'd just eaten a piece of green fruit, the clergyman reiterated, "Do you, Diantha Maria Fraser, take this man for your lawfully wedded husband?"

Diantha tried to swallow, but her mouth was bone dry. "I . . . I do."

"Repeat after me . . ."

Like a sleepwalker, she stumbled

through her responses. Only the rich resonance of Sebastian's voice as he promised to love, honour and cherish her made an impression. Before she knew it, he'd slipped a gold wedding band on her finger.

"I now pronounce you man and wife!" proclaimed the clergyman. He rearranged his features in an odd-looking smirk that Diantha supposed would pass for a smile in a pinch.

Sebastian raised her veil and looked at her solemnly for several nerve-wracking heartbeats. Then Crawford, who'd viewed the ceremony from a front pew, gave a watery sniffle that forced Diantha to recognize she hadn't dreamed the exchangement of vows. For better or worse, she was well and truly married.

In late afternoon of the second day of their journey, the coach and four rattled through the wrought-iron archway that marked the entrance to Ravistock's Wiltshire estate. Diantha caught a whiff of roses laced with honeysuckle wafting from a tangle of overgrown vines that partially obscured the open gate's delicate filigree pattern.

"Umm," she murmured in rapt appreciation. "The mingling of scents is divine."

Sebastian's gaze held frank admiration.

Two days on the road would tire the most seasoned traveller. Yet, there sat his bride, wide-eyed and eager, and looking crisp and cool in a navy spencer worn over a blue-and-white-striped polished cotton dress, donned before breakfast at a coaching inn where they'd spent the night.

He smiled. How lovely she'd looked at their wedding in her off-white silk gown embellished with Brussels lace. Still he'd been right to decree she needn't wear mourning here in the country.

"Look sharp, my love! Teale Manor is about to come into view."

Shading her eyes, Diantha squinted into the sun. The manor was faced with faded brick with occasional blue "burnt" headers to add variety. As the coachman pulled to a stop, she saw that the front door was crowned with an arched pediment adorned with mythical creatures. The curved motif was repeated in unusual white semicircles suspended above the front windows which created an illusion of raised eyebrows and gave the house an air of perpetual surprise.

Sebastian disembarked first, then handed his bride down. Awaiting them on the doorstep was a middle-aged couple.

"My love, this is the housekeeper, Mrs. Twicket."

Diantha returned the housekeeper's nod. "And this is Brimble."

The butler bowed and declared himself honoured to be at her service.

"Are the rest of the staff lined up indoors?" Sebastian asked Brimble.

"Aye, my lord. I'll warrant every man-Jack and Jill of the lot is eager for a glimpse of your marchioness."

"In that case, we mustn't disappoint them."

Diantha's grip on her husband's arm tightened as he led her inside. The fact that the front hall rose upwards to a vaulted ceiling and boasted a salmon-coloured marble floor barely had time to register before she sighted two rows of servants: men to her right; women to her left. Her heart plummeted. How on earth would she ever learn to manage such a large staff? she wondered as Sebastian signalled a shy young maid to step forward.

"My dear, this is Katie. She'll serve as your abigail during our stay."

A protest hovered on the tip of Diantha's tongue. Wisely, she squelched it. She'd been on the verge of saying she didn't require a lady's maid, when she realised a marchioness would be expected to employ one. How bothersome!

"Pleased I be to serve your ladyship." Katie bobbed a curtsey and stepped back into place.

It wasn't long before Diantha's head began to swim and she lost all track of the servants' names. Sebastian gave his bride a shrewd look. "Mrs. Twicket, be so good as to show the marchioness to her suite. I daresay a short rest will revive her. Diantha, would you join me in the library in two hours."

The housekeeper seemed efficient, Diantha conceded as they climbed the stairs. Still she missed Crawfy. Bidding her former nanny Godspeed immediately after the ceremony at St. George's had been heartwrenching. However, Crawford had always planned to spend her declining years with her sister in Sussex. Now that Diantha no longer needed a chaperone, it would have been monstrously selfish to ask her to postpone her retirement any longer.

Twicket ushered Diantha into an attractive bedchamber. All the furniture was painted a pale peach, which subtly contrasted with the scalloped-edged canopy curtain and matching dust ruffle done up in cream satin.

"The Feather Suite, your ladyship."

Diantha glanced about the room. "Nary

a feather. How curious."

"It's so named because of all the plumes."

Careful study revealed that carved plumes topped off each bedpost. Noting that the delicate plume motif also embellished the wooden moulding of the canopy frame and was repeated in the side chairs, Diantha murmured in an amused tone of voice, "I shouldn't wonder."

"There's a sitting room. Would you care to see it?"

"How can I resist?" Diantha awarded the housekeeper a bright smile. Espying a door cut into a side wall, she headed towards it.

"Not that door, my lady," Twicket cautioned. "That one leads into the master's suite."

Diantha froze in her tracks. Fanning hot cheeks, she wished she weren't so impulsive.

"This way, my lady."

Diantha followed the housekeeper into the adjacent room. There, she was elated to find the plume motif and peach and cream colour had been carried over into her private parlor.

When she returned to the bedroom, Katie, who had hurried up the backstairs with a hot can of water, was waiting patiently. Diantha assured the servants she had everything she required and dismissed them. When she had washed her hands and face and lain down on the comfortable bed, she surprised herself by falling asleep at once.

Refreshed by her nap, Diantha stood at the foot of the stairs. She espied an oval mirror against gold flocked wallpaper and hurried to it. In her anxiety not to be late, she'd forgotten to glance at her reflection before rushing from her suite. But now, peering into the glass, she was relieved to see that Katie had done her hair up a fair treat.

Raised male voices drifted from a room whose double doors were propped open. Intrigued, Diantha sallied forth.

"I tell you, Will, there's something havey-cavey about this wedding."

"Don't be daft, Harry. Uncle's been on the town for years. He's up to every rig and row."

"Rubbish! Married the chit by special license, didn't he? Affair's as queer as Dick's hatband."

"Hold your jaw, Harry, 'afore you make a regular Jack Pudding of yourself. Why the way you go on, you'd think you were the one who just got leg shackled — instead of your older brother."

"Exactly my point! No one would raise an eyebrow if I'd as good as eloped, cause I'm known for cutting up larks."

Poised on the threshold, Diantha said frostily. "I trust I don't intrude."

Harry colored to the roots of his hair, but before she could deliver the setdown he richly deserved, Sebastian was at her side, cupping her elbow in his hand.

"My love, this is my brother, Harry, and my nephew, Will Bentley. Boys, make your bows to my wife, Diantha."

In their mad scramble to obey, the two youths managed to bump heads. The disgruntled expression on both their faces struck Diantha as comical. She barely stifled a giggle.

"One at a time!" Sebastian barked.

First Will, then Harry, made her an elegant leg and assured her they were charmed to make her acquaintance.

"Silly young cawkers," Sebastian grumbled once they'd subsided.

Unable to contain her amusement any longer, Diantha dissolved into a fit of the giggles. Sebastian regarded her with undisguised fondness. He liked hearing her laugh. Besides, Harry's and Will's antics were amusing. The corners of his mouth lifted and his shoulders shook. Then, losing his tenuous grasp on his composure, he threw back his head and gave a roar of laughter.

Harry and Will stared at the newlyweds, exchanged a shrug, and ended up with droll grins.

Carrying in the tea tray laden with cream buns and apricot tarts, Brimble permitted himself the briefest of smiles. It had been years since he'd heard Master Sebastian laugh like that. Brimble fancied himself an excellent judge of character, and, unless he missed his guess, the new marchioness was the very lady to turn his lordship up sweet.

Chapter 9

Eyes closed, Diantha gave herself up to the steady, rhythmic strokes of a brush being slowly pulled through her hair by her abigail. She'd almost succeeded into lulling herself into a tranquil frame of mind when a rap on the outer door shattered her composure.

"C— come in," she stammered.

Much on his dignity, Brimble entered, bearing a bottle of vintage champagne. Behind him a footman carried in a tray brimming with covered dishes.

Diantha glanced at her peach satin *negligee* worn over a matching bedgown. Its sheerness caused her to blush. Even though Brimble didn't so much as turn a hair, she was not at all certain it was proper for male servants to enter, considering her state of *dishabille*.

Pride stiffened her backbone. It would never do to reveal her misgivings. She quirked an eyebrow. "What's all this?"

"Your wedding supper, my lady,"

155

Brimble replied, his expression bland. "The master thinks you'll be more comfortable dining informally here in your suite."

"I see," she said faintly.

Brimble placed the champagne on a small round table near French doors that opened onto a balcony. After the footman had finished arranging the silver and china to the eagle-eyed butler's satisfaction, both servants bowed and took themselves off.

Katie set the silver-backed hairbrush on the dressing table. "Will that be all, my lady?"

Diantha stirred uneasily. To be candid, she was reluctant to dismiss her abigail. But a moment's quiet reflection made her see that such hen-hearted behaviour wouldn't answer. The Marchioness of Ravistock must not hide behind her maid's skirts! To sustain herself, Diantha drew a deep breath.

"Yes, Katie, you may go."

Nonetheless, the instant she was alone, Diantha's *sangfroid* deserted her. Any second, her husband would walk through the connecting door. And then what? Overset, she dug her fingernails into her palm. How could she ever hope to measure up to Honoria in Sebastian's eyes? Particularly when she had only the sketchiest notion of what was about to occur.

Wincing, she unclasped her hands. Would Sebastian hold her appalling ignorance against her? She stared unseeingly at the grooves embedded in her palms.

With a sigh, she arose and drifted through open French doors onto a wrought-iron balcony that overlooked a garden. An intriguing meld of sweet fragrances spiralled upwards from a muddled profusion of flowers sharing the same bed. To divert her mind from her problems, she identified the peonies, Canterbury bells, and sweet William interspersed amongst climbing roses and white clematis.

Feeling calmer, Diantha retreated back into her bedchamber. There, the tantalizing smells emanating from the laden table drew her. She lifted the lid of one of the covered dishes. Roast duck in orange sauce made her mouth water.

The sound of a turning doorknob caused her to give a small start. Eyes glued to the connecting door that led to the master suite, Diantha held her breath.

"May I come in?"

Hearing no demurral, Sebastian entered, whistling softly. However, one glance at his bride's face sobered him. "My dear, I am not an ogre."

"I . . . I know. It's just that I'm so . . . nervous."

With a reassuring smile, Sebastian held out his hand. "Come sit with me, my love, and tell me what troubles you," he coaxed. "There should be no secrets between man and wife."

Talking soothingly, he led her over to a wing chair. He lowered himself into its generous depths, then settled her upon his lap. Diantha made a feeble attempt to scramble off, but his grasp remained firm. He scanned her face for a minute, then gave a soft chuckle.

"My lovely rosy-cheeked bride. Has my boldness put you to the blush?"

Eyes demurely downcast, she mumbled, "I fear I'll disappoint you. I don't know what to do, what to expect."

"Ah," he said, his demeanour clearing as understanding dawned.

But mere seconds later, his momentary sanguinity took wing as he faced the truth. Although he now knew the problem, he had no idea of how best to proceed.

His brow wrinkled as he pondered his dilemma. True, he'd never had the least bit of trouble dealing with the fair sex before — Honoria included. However, past experience was of no help to him now. Diantha was neither a bit of muslin nor a bored noblewoman interested in dalliance. On the contrary, his bride was a complete innocent. To make matters worse, she was an orphan with no mother to advise her. *No wonder she's as nervous as a high-strung filly,* he thought.

"Did Crawford talk to you about tonight?" Sebastian asked.

Diantha shook her head. "Crawfy only said that my husba . . . that you would instruct me."

"I see." Sebastian smothered a sigh. Beads of perspiration dotted his forehead.

Diantha noted his discomfiture. The growing realization she wasn't the only one who was worried lifted her spirits.

She awarded him a shy smile and, taking hold of the lapel of his Persian-style dressing gown, rubbed her thumb lightly across the cool silk.

"I'm unfamiliar with this pattern," she confided huskily. "Do you know what it's called?"

"P— paisley," he stammered, both stunned and charmed by her boldness.

Devil a bit! Was it possible Diantha was bent on seducing him? A lazy smile animated his features. What a diverting thought!

"Milord, with all the delicious aromas floating in the air, are you not the least bit curious about supper?"

He bit back a chuckle. Here was a facer. While he dreamt of being sweetly seduced, his bride suffered hunger pangs.

He flashed her a crooked grin. "Hungry?"

"Famished!" she confessed artlessly.

Still smiling, he playfully tweaked Diantha's small, straight nose. "In that case, shall we see what the cook sent up for our wedding supper?"

Seated at the table, Sebastian took pains to hide his amusement as he watched Diantha pile food upon a Sevres china plate. Addressing his more modest selection, he found the roast duck succulent. Nonetheless, once he'd taken the edge off his appetite, he felt obliged to return to his ruminations. After all, the problem of how to enlighten his bride was not resolved — only postponed.

Diantha glanced up from her plate to cast him a demure look. "Are you certain you will not sample the trifle? Upon my word, it's excellent."

"No, thank you, my love." He schooled

himself to wait patiently until she'd scraped the last bit of sweet cream from her dish and set down her spoon.

Sebastian cleared his throat. "My dear, I confess I am at somewhat of a loss."

"My lord, if you'd rather not explain, I won't tease you."

"Not at all. I shall be pleased to elucidate." *Once I hit upon the right words,* he thought glumly.

Such an awesome responsibility weighed heavily upon him. Out of consideration for his bride's sensibilities, Sebastian had refrained from approaching Diantha en route to Teale Manor. Now, he wondered if he should put off the consummation of their marriage yet again. No, he decided, the longer he postponed his bride's initiation into conjugal bliss, the more awkward their situation would become.

Besides, he'd give odds Diantha was at present more comfortable than he was. Anyway, he was tired of trying to untangle his tongue. Far easier to demonstrate.

Pulling her to her feet, Sebastian enveloped her in a fervent embrace. At first, Diantha was too startled to respond, but gradually the gentle persuasion of his lips grew fiercer. Somewhere deep inside her, the dam holding her natural responses in check burst. With a long sigh of surrender, she melted against his hard, lean frame. However it was not until he renewed his tender assault on her sweet mouth that Diantha tumbled into a vortex of pleasurable sensations that banished all lingering vestiges of fear . . . all thought.

The marquess opened his eyes. Sunlight streamed from the tall windows. As objects came into focus, a silly, fatuous grin spread across Sebastian's face. Last night. . . . He sighed. Such a momentous experience. He glanced at his bride, still fast asleep. A tender smile softened his aristocratic features as he watched the slight rise and fall of her chest. In the glow of last night's candlelight, her cloud of raven hair swirling about her ivory face and shoulders had made her seem ethereal . . . a vision almost certain to vanish with the dawn.

Thus, Sebastian was gratified to discover that in the cold light of day, Diantha looked even lovelier. Unable to resist her allure any longer, he reached out and touched a lock of hair resting upon a satin pillow.

By heaven, last night had been wondrous fine! Were he a selfish man, he'd rouse Diantha from sleep with ardent kisses. But no, she needed her rest. He must be patient. He would be patient. Patience had certainly paid off the previous evening. Besides, it was not just Diantha's body he coveted. He wanted all of her, her thoughts, her affections, her devotion . . . the very essence of her.

What's more, he refused to be satisfied with anything less, he decided as he shrugged into his dressing gown and tiptoed from his wife's room. Closing the connecting door gently, he acknowledged that if anyone had told him a month ago that he was on the brink of falling hopelessly in love with his ward, he would have scoffed. However, that is exactly what had happened. Life was certainly full of surprises. What he needed was a brisk gallop on his stallion to clear the cobwebs from his mind, Sebastian reflected as he rang for his valet.

Diantha awoke with a start. Disoriented, she was only dimly aware that someone was knocking on the hall door.

"Who is it?" she murmured, her husky voice raspy from sleep.

"Katie, my lady."

"Oh, Katie. Do come in."

"The door's locked, my lady."

Strange, Diantha thought, sitting up abruptly. She did not recall locking it. She started to scramble out of the tangled bedclothes when one of her hands chanced to brush against her bare thigh. She felt herself flush from head to toe. Last night, she and Sebastian . . . Words failed her.

As memory of the previous evening spent in her husband's arms became more vivid, Diantha placed cool fingertips on her burning cheeks. But, once her embarrassment had run its course, a sweet smile curved her mouth as she recalled how gentle and loving Sebastian had been. Without a doubt, she was fortunate to have such a considerate husband.

Seized by a sudden desire to observe what he looked like when asleep, Diantha cast a sidelong glance. Although she could still see the indentation where his head had rested, Sebastian himself was gone. She was intensely disappointed.

"My lady, I have your breakfast. . . ."

Jerked back to the present by her abigail's plight, Diantha called, "I'm coming. Just give me a minute."

She spotted her bedgown thrown across the back of one of the boudoir chairs. She slipped it over her head and crossed to the threshold. After turning the key in the lock, Diantha stepped out of the way just as the hall door swung inward to admit the maid.

"Be you wishful of eating in bed, my lady, or at the table?"

"The table. No, wait . . ." Diantha looked flustered. "I'd forgotten. It hasn't been cleared yet."

"Only take me a minute, my lady."

True to her word, Katie set down the tray and walked over to the round table. Quickly, she stacked the dishes and cutlery and carried them out into the hall. Returning, she deposited the breakfast tray on the table and opened the French doors.

"The birds be singing and the coffee be hot. Enjoy your meal, my lady."

"I'm certain I shall. And Katie, I desire a bath. Would you be so kind as to have hot water brought up?"

"That I will, my lady."

"Thank you, Katie. I'll ring for you when I've finished my breakfast."

The coffee was strong. Not that Diantha minded. The bracing drink was just what she needed. As she tapped the soft-boiled egg with her spoon, her mood turned pensive. She so wished Sebastian had awakened her before he'd left. It would have been such a comfort if he'd been the first thing she'd seen upon opening her eyes. Last night, he'd been so tender that he'd made her feel cherished.

Even so, since Sebastian had left her without a word this morning, it was possible the experience they'd shared had affected her more deeply than it had him.

Diantha dipped a toast point into the yolk of her egg. While true she was not worldly, she'd always felt she had good instincts. If she trusted them now, she must take care not to hang on her husband's sleeve, however much she longed to share every waking minute with him. Nothing would make him lose patience with her more quickly.

She must hold his interest, whatever the cost. She loved him too much to lose him to another. She wanted to be more than his wife . . . more than the mother of his children. She wanted to be everything to him.

Thank goodness they were on their honeymoon. If they were still in London, he might be tempted to stray back into Lady Fitzwilliam's arms. But they weren't in town, they were in Wiltshire, far from that particular temptation. Moreover, Diantha intended to use every womanly wile at her command to engage her husband's affections.

Sebastian peered up into the sky, calculating the time by the position of the sun. Around four o'clock, he conceded gloomily. He nudged his sleek roan stallion towards Teale Manor.

When he'd left Diantha still asleep that morning, he'd intended only to take Merlin for a vigourous gallop, returning in time to join his bride in the breakfast room. It was while he was walking the stallion to cool him down that he'd spotted the cottage where his old nurse resided. Recalling that Brimble had mentioned that Mrs. Williams had been ailing of late, he'd decided to pay her a short visit.

Unhappily for Sebastian's good intentions, the instant he'd stepped into Annie Williams's whitewashed cottage, his plans began to go awry.

His former nurse had greeted him with a pleased cackle and ordered him in a tone that brooked no nonsense, "Sit yourself down, Master Sebastian. I'll slice you a piece of apple cake."

Sebastian felt torn. He knew he shouldn't take the time, but to refuse would hurt her feelings. Besides, he'd acknowledged with a rueful grin, he'd never been able to resist Nurse's apple cake.

He was eating a second helping when Annie Williams wagged her finger at him and admonished, "Shame on you, Master Sebastian, for letting that sweet innocent you married wake up alone in a strange household."

Chagrined, Sebastian began to eat faster. "You're right of course. I deserve the firing squad for my thoughtlessness. Rest assured I'll make it up to her."

"See that you do," she grumbled. "And don't you dare gobble my apple cake!"

It was perhaps fortunate that he left the cottage so stuffed, he'd had no appetite come noontime. For just outside, he'd been waylaid by his estate manager. It seemed his prize bull had kicked down the south pasture fence and escaped into his neighbour's field. Since Sebastian had paid a great deal for the animal, and had high hopes of using it to help build up his herd, prompt recovery was essential. Especially as he knew Squire Western was likely to order the recalcitrant bovine shot on sight. Under the circumstances, he'd felt compelled to accompany his steward.

Now, dismounting in the stable yard, Sebastian ruefully shook his head. He'd expected to return much earlier, but recovery of the unruly bull and calming his irate neighbour by promising to compensate him for his trampled corn had taken up a large chunk of time. As he handed the reins over to a young undergroom and headed toward the manor, he hoped Diantha hadn't felt too neglected.

Entering through the kitchen, Sebastian went to the library and was about to ring for Brimble and enquire as to Diantha's whereabouts when Harry's boisterous shout drew him to the room's French doors. He chuckled at the sight that met his eyes. Just beyond the Yorkstone terrace on a wide expanse of lawn, Harry, Will, and Diantha were playing Battledore. Or, to be strictly accurate, Will, his hornbook-shaped racket lowered, looked on with interest while Harry and Diantha battled each other for the shuttlecock.

Sebastian grinned. Such fun, he thought, tempted to join them. He sobered. Best not. The three of them were cavorting like children. No doubt his presence would put a damper on their carefree abandon.

A hesitant smile lit his face. Her cheeks rosy from wholesome exertion, Diantha was the picture of health and grace as she vied with Harry for the shuttlecock. Furthermore, she looked charming in her sprigged muslin gown, perfect for an unseasonably warm May afternoon.

A sharp pang of envy caused Sebastian to turn abruptly away from the diverting scene. He strolled over to the bookshelves. He pulled out a book at random, skimmed the first page, then returned it to its proper slot with a sigh. He wasn't in the mood.

Once again, his brother's high pitched voice filtered through the terrace doors. Oh the devil! Instead of sulking, why not join them as he was longing to do? Come to that, only seven years separated himself and his bride. Those few years scarcely qualified him for the part of Methuselah.

Sebastian opened one of the doors and stepped onto the terrace. He was moving toward the lawn at a moderate clip when a sickening crack brought him to a halt. Bad enough that their rackets collided, causing Harry's to snap off at the top of the handle. Potentially more serious, the two combatants had bumped heads. Harry reeled, but kept to his feet. Pulses pounding, Sebastian scarcely noticed since his eyes were riveted upon Diantha as she pitched backwards onto the lawn.

For a horrifying second, sheer terror

squeezed the air from his lungs. Then Diantha gave a peal of laughter. To Sebastian, it was the most welcome sound he'd ever heard. Yet, paradoxically, fear turned to fury as he rushed forwards. Shunting his brother aside, he knelt on the lawn next to his bride, who'd managed to assume a sitting position. Grasping her gently by the shoulders, he stared deep into her eyes.

"Dearest, are you all right?"

Diantha answered with a spontaneous giggle. Covering her mouth, she scrambled to her feet and dusted off the grass-stained skirt of her gown.

"It was a mere tempest in a teacup," she informed him airily. "We were involved in a spirited game of Battledore when we crashed into each other."

Sebastian struggled to keep a firm rein on his temper. "My love, I'm glad you escaped serious harm. Just the same I mean to have a word with Harry."

He glanced around, intending to take his brother to task for playing so roughly with a delicately reared female, but both Harry and Will had vanished. Not that he blamed those two scamps. He'd charged across the lawn like an enraged bull. A reluctant smile twitched at the edges of his mouth.

Very astute of Harry to make himself scarce until Sebastian's anger cooled.

After escorting Diantha to the door of her suite, he advised her to ring for Katie. "You can rest until it is time for her to make you presentable for dinner."

"I will," she agreed. As he started to move away, she touched his arm, causing him to gaze at her quizzically. "Sebastian, don't be too hard on your brother. I hadn't seen you all day. He was just trying to cheer me up."

Guilt abraded his conscience like a hair shirt. Here he'd been blaming Harry for what had occurred when he was equally at fault.

Sebastian grazed Diantha's smooth cheek lightly with his knuckles. "Don't worry, sweet. My bark's worse than my bite."

"You're no longer angry?"

Expression wry, he shook his head. "To tell the truth, I was jealous."

"Jealous? You?" She eyed him searchingly.

Looking sheepish, he confessed, "I can't say I blame you for being incredulous. Until today, jealousy and I were strangers. I must say it's a disconcerting sensation."

"Isn't it just," she commiserated. "I experienced a nasty jolt at the opera."

"Did you, dearest?" The specter of Honoria seemed to hang in the air between them. Sebastian gently cupped Diantha's chin, forcing her to meet his compelling gaze. "No need to be jealous. I've severed the connection."

Diantha gave a long, heartfelt sigh. "Are you certain? Her ladyship is so sophisticated. Last night, I feared I might bore you."

He grinned. "Minx! Fishing for compliments, I vow! Suffice it to say our wedding night was an experience I shall always treasure."

Diantha's face grew radiant. "Truly? When I woke up this morning and found you gone, I feared I'd failed to measure up," she confided.

Sebastian could kick himself for making Diantha unhappy. He gazed at her earnestly. "Listen to me. If a man wants an experienced partner to share his bed, it's easy to come by. Marriage is not at all necessary."

"Are you saying you married me for my innocence, rather than in spite of it?"

Sebastian sighed. "That's one way of putting it, I suppose. The point I wish to make is that you could never bore me. As a matter of fact, last night I found your naivete a sheer delight."

Diantha wrinkled her nose. "But if that's what you value so highly, doesn't it follow . . . ? I'm confused."

"That makes two of us," he observed wryly.

"This is very awkward," Diantha confessed. "What I intended to ask is, now that I'm no longer a green girl, won't you be bored?"

She's dead serious, Sebastian realised, endeavouring to keep a straight face. Alas, he could not prevent his shoulders from shaking. Finally, he gave up and roared with laughter.

Diantha stared at him in puzzlement. Recovering his composure, he cast her a bemused smile.

"Sweetheart, you are an incurable innocent. A thousand nights — nay a million — spent in your arms will make no difference. No, my love, I will never tire of you."

"Sebastian," Diantha murmured dreamily, then gave a sigh of contentment as Sebastian enveloped her in a tender embrace. "Perhaps you should rest also?"

Chapter 10

As his travel coach rumbled into Bishop's Canning, the marquess, features set in a ferocious scowl, stared out the window.

"Damn and blast" he exclaimed.

Yesterday, a courier had arrived from London with an urgent message. The First Lord of the Admiralty had apologised for interrupting his honeymoon but begged him come posthaste.

Sebastian hadn't wanted to leave Diantha behind. Yet, the admiral had stated his presence would be needed only for a few days — a sennight at most. Under the circumstances, it would have been unpardonably foolish — not to mention selfish — to drag his bride up to town for such a short span of time.

He sighed. The truth was he himself resented having to leave Teale Manor. He'd been so happy there. During the entire month of May, he'd felt as if he and Diantha had fallen under a spell of enchantment.

Simple pleasures had taken on a new aura. Most days had begun with Diantha's riding lesson. While still a bit skittish in the saddle, she'd worked hard to overcome her fears. Her spunk was an admirable trait, in her husband's estimation.

A soft smile curved his mouth. It was the afternoons he'd miss the most. Afternoons reserved for the two of them. Sometimes they'd taken the gig to Bishop's Canning, where Diantha had struck up a promising acquaintance with the Reverend David Chase's wife, Charity. Sometimes they'd ventured an extra three miles to Devizes to take tea at the Bear Inn and watch the London stage en route to Bath whiz past. Other times they'd gone rowing, or visited the home farm, or stopped to drink tea with Annie Williams. Above all, he'd enjoyed their picnics, always in some secluded spot of his choosing.

His smile faded as he recalled the problems facing him at the Admiralty. Thanks to the recent unrest in Spain and Portugal, Parliament was debating the wisdom of ordering the Fleet to the Mediterranean. His counsel was needed and, in the event that the proposal carried, his knack for organisation.

The marquess's expression grew wistful. No more picnics for two — at least not until his return.

"Damn and blast!" he reiterated.

Two days later, Diantha stared at the swatch of striped olive and gold satin in her hand, trying to visualise how it would look made up to cover the entire sofa. With new wallpaper and gold window hangings, it might prove rather striking, she decided.

A teardrop splashed her hand. Quickly, she brushed it aside. Goose! she mentally chided. No point in making a Cheltenham tragedy over their first separation. Still, it hurt that he'd left her behind. Clearly, he did not want a wife who lived in his pocket. But it was childish to repine. He'd be back before she knew it. What's more, the time would pass more swiftly if she kept busy.

With the latter thought in mind, she'd made herself concentrate on the redecorating scheme she'd embarked on with her husband's permission. Yesterday she'd persuaded Harry to escort her to Devizes. There an obliging draper provided her with sample swatches to help her make up her mind as to which fabrics to buy.

Furthermore, when Sebastian had asked her if she had any commission she wished him to undertake while in town, she'd snipped a bit of blue silk brocade from the underside of the Chippendale chairs in the dining room. He'd promised to do his best to match it, though perhaps he'd be too busy with Admiralty affairs. If that should prove to be the case, she'd resolved not to tax him with it. Indeed, she missed Sebastian so much, she'd be content with his prompt return. Without him beside her, the magic had vanished from her days.

Halting at the crest of the hill so their mounts could catch their breath, Harry turned to Diantha. "High time we headed back to the stables."

"Could we not continue a trifle farther?" she coaxed.

He laughed. "Stop trying to turn me up sweet, Di. Save your womanly wiles for Sebastian."

With a sigh, Diantha wheeled her horse round. As they made for home, Harry could see she was blue-devilled and felt obliged to cheer her up.

"Speaking of my brother, I wager he'll be happy as a grig when he sees how well you manage your mare. And just wait until he sees you handle the ribbons of my curricle."

A wistful expression came into Diantha's eyes. "Appears to me he's forgotten I exist."

"Gammon! Depend upon it, Sebastian'd be here with you if he could. He's heels over head in love."

"Fustian! Three and a half weeks have passed, Harry. He said he'd be gone a sennight at most. Furthermore, except for a few lines he sent just after he arrived, h— he hasn't even bothered to w— write." Mortified by the break in her voice, she clamped her mouth shut.

"Here now, Di, don't take on so. The navy brass keep him too busy to write."

"Your loyalty to your brother does you credit, but I beg leave to doubt it!" Overset, Diantha dug her booted heel into the mare's flank, spurring her mount to a canter.

"Di, mind what you're about!"

Diantha heard Harry's warning shout, but was too overwrought to heed him. When her common sense finally reasserted itself, Diantha drew back on the reins. To her horror, the mare ignored the signal to slacken her speed. As they shot past the whitewashed cottages, the phrase "pride goeth before a fall" popped into Diantha's mind. Hysterical laughter bubbled forth. Was she about to pay for her folly literally by parting company with her mount?

Happily, as they neared the stables, the winded mare slowed of her own accord. With a final burst of energy, her exhausted mistress managed a weak tug on the reins. To her surprise, the horse came to a halt.

A young stable boy rushed forward to assist the dishevelled marchioness from her saddle. The head groom waylaid her before she could escape the stableyard. "Could've broken your neck, ma'am. 'Sides, that be no way to treat fine horseflesh."

Ashamed of herself, Diantha hung her head. "I'm sorry, Ben, I . . ."

Harry rode in and dismounted. "Of all the feather-witted starts! I've a good mind to wash my hands of you."

"I shan't blame you if you do," said Diantha quietly. "Only . . . I hope you'll give me another chance. I so want to please Sebastian with my progress."

"Please Sebastian! I've a good mind to write and tell him what a fool you've been."

"No, Harry — you can't." It was enough

that her husband neglected her. Far too much if her brother-in-law washed his hands of her, too.

"All right, Di, if you promise to be more careful."

"Oh, I do. I do!"

"La, Sebastian, you naughty rogue, where have you been hiding?"

The marquess halted in his tracks, his expression sardonic as he spotted Honoria poised in front of a marble caryatid — one of many that graced several alcoves interspersed along the edges of the ballroom.

Though it was the tail end of June and the Season was at its height, Ravistock had deliberately eschewed the social scene. Curst bad luck that, the first time he ventured abroad, he'd been cornered by his tenacious former mistress. If only Petersham had not asked him to drop in at the comeout ball of his Leicester cousins and do his possible to add to their consequence, Sebastian might have continued to avoid this unwelcome confrontation. Indeed, having danced with each young lady in turn, he'd been about to bid *adieu* to his hostess, but now the fat was in the fire — for here stood Honoria.

Quelling a sigh, Sebastian dutifully

bowed over the hand her ladyship extended. Straightening, he said, "I haven't been hiding, Lady Fitzwilliam. I've been up to my eyes in paperwork at the Admiralty."

"Fie, sir, it was most ungallant of you not to answer my notes." She emphasized her remark by lightly rapping his knuckles with her closed fan.

He gave a lazy shrug. "As I said, I've been busy."

Awarding him her most charming smile, Honoria gently tugged on his sleeve. "Waltz with me, and all is forgiven."

Why not? Sebastian thought. Desirous of ending their *tête-à-tête* in the relatively secluded alcove before tongues began to wag, he gave a cool nod.

"Madam, your magnanimity overwhelms me."

As he led her onto the crowded ballroom floor, he felt quite the clever fellow. However, his smugness was short-lived. For no sooner had they begun to waltz than Honoria proceeded to behave like a trollop.

Slyly pressing her voluptuous body close to his own, she murmured in his ear. "Lud, I've missed you!"

"Behave yourself, madam!" Sebastian

cautioned, taking a step backwards.

To no avail, for, once again, she snuggled up to him. As he whirled past a row of seated old biddies, beads of perspiration dotted his forehead. Appalled, grimly determined not to cause a scandal if he could help it, he was obliged to employ his superior strength to maintain the proper distance between them.

"My lord, you look a trifle . . . discomposed. It is overwarm in here. Perhaps a walk on the terrace would prove mutually beneficial," Honoria purred.

Devil a bit! Did the jade think him so easily manoeuvred? Deciding it was imperative he escape from her toils before she pulled something really outrageous, he said silkily, "I've a much better idea."

Honoria giggled. "Tell all, naughty boy."

With an enigmatic smile, he waltzed her back to the alcove where he'd first encountered her.

"Wait here, madam, while I procure you a glass of lemonade. It is sure to cool you off." Ignoring Honoria's disgruntled gasp, Sebastian strode blithely away.

As he walked to the refreshment table, he collared Petersham. "Come along with me, Charles. I require your assistance."

"What's this all about?" the viscount

asked after a footman presiding over the tempting buffet gave Ravistock the lemonade he requested.

Smiling, Sebastian handed Petersham the glass. "One good turn deserves another. Since I showed up to dance attendance at the comeout of your relatives, the least you can do is deliver lemonade to Honoria and butter her up while I slip away."

Petersham laughed. "Trying to sink her tentacles into you again, is she?" The amusement in his eyes was replaced by wary caution as he deftly probed, "My lady is very lovely. Are you certain you wish to be rid of her?"

"Very certain. I'm a married man."

"So pleased you remember. I had wondered since you left your wife in Wiltshire. Your bride is a delightful creature."

"So she is. As for Honoria, if you are so taken with her charms, pray don't hesitate on my account."

"I appreciate your frankness. Do excuse me. I'm off to deliver a glass of lemonade and try my luck."

As soon as Petersham had melted into the crowd, the marquess wasted no time locating his hostess and taking his leave.

The morning after her wild horseback

ride, Diantha awoke to find a blanket of fog had descended during the night. Though the change of weather depressed her, she was not about to give in to flagging spirits. A soft moan escaped her as she tossed back the covers and attempted to rise. The price of yesterday's willful canter was very dear indeed, she acknowledged as she lifted her aching arm to pull the bell cord.

My word! Diantha thought as she sipped her morning chocolate. Even the bones in her wrist ached when she lifted the delicate porcelain cup. In fact, all her bones felt brittle. What's more, the clammy dampness seemed to seep into her very marrow. If only the sun would break through the dense fog.

After Katie helped her struggle into a long-sleeved dress of slate blue merino, Diantha ambled slowly down the stairs and into the music room. When her fingers had warmed up, she sang a few notes, then stopped and looked around guiltily.

Diantha gave a deep sigh. She missed singing in the church choir so much. How she wished she could make Sebastian understand how important singing was to her. And why hadn't he written her? Had he really been summoned to town by the

Admiralty? Her nimble fingers went from a gay sonatina to the ponderous chords of an andante movement of a concerto. Or had it been a ploy to keep her buried in the country while he resumed his affair with Honoria?

Diantha hit a discordant note. Her hands stilled on the keyboard. In the throes of despair, her eyes swam with tears.

John Coachman turned off Bath Road a mile or so after passing through Bishop's Canning.

"Humph! Village appears the same as it did last time I visited," boomed the dowager Marchioness of Ravistock.

"I'm not surprised. It seldom changes," observed her daughter, Lady Jane.

"True enough. But what with that . . . that . . . by-blow installed at Teale Manor, who knows in what state we'd find it?"

"Really, Mama! Did you truly think your daughter-in-law could manage to set the neighborhood on its ears in the space of a few weeks?"

The dowager's homely features set in a mulish expression. "Weeks? Months more like," she scoffed.

Mama's bent on mischief! Lady Jane silently lamented. What a pity her crony,

Lady Dalrymple, had received that letter crammed with the latest *ton* gossip from her niece in London. But for that unhappy event, Mama wouldn't have known Sebastian was in town without his bride.

"Do try for a little sense, Jane," the dowager advised sarcastically. "The gel's a fast worker. Managed to lure Sebastian to the altar quicker than a cat could lick its ear, didn't she?"

"You are being very unfair. Now that she's part of the family, don't you think you ought to make an effort to accept her?"

"Maria Fraser's baseborn brat? Never!"

"If that's how you feel, far better we stayed in Bath. Sebastian will not thank you for upsetting his wife."

"Ha! If that were the case, he wouldn't have deserted her. Mark my words, he regrets marrying the chit. Not that he'll ever admit he made a mistake. Too stubborn by far! Upon my word, I can't imagine how he came by such a disagreeable trait. No doubt he takes after his father's side of the family in that respect."

Lady Jane heaved a great sigh. "For your sake, I hope you don't anger Sebastian."

"I trust I know my own son," the dowager said in an affronted tone of voice. "No doubt he'll thank me for squashing the chit's pretensions."

Lady Jane winced. The echoing of her mother's stentorian voice in the confined space of the closed carriage was making her head throb.

"Have it your way, Mama," she said, retiring from the lists.

"I fully intend to," thundered the dowager, girding up for the impending battle.

Chapter 11

The ancient carriage pulled up before Teale Manor, and a postboy was dispatched to alert the household of its arrival. Brimble responded to the door-knocker with alacrity. Recognizing the boy's green and gold livery, he hurried outside and down stone steps to greet the dowager marchioness, who'd emerged from the coach with the aid of one of her footmen.

"Your ladyship, this is an unexpected pleasure. The instant we enter the manor, I shall inform her ladyship," Brimble advised.

"Time enough to meet her later," boomed the dowager marchioness. "I prefer to settle in first."

"In that case, my lady, I shall instruct Twicket to air a suite."

"I trust you won't try and fob me off with just any bedchamber. Well you know, I prefer the Feather Suite."

Brimble turned red as a radish. "Much

as I'd like to oblige your ladyship, I fear that's impossible. The master himself assigned those rooms to his bride."

Assuming the pose of a long-suffering martyr, the dowager spoke in a carrying tone of voice that would have done Mrs. Siddons proud. "That my own flesh and blood would serve me such a trick! Brimble, I have nurtured a viper at my breast."

"Indeed, my lady."

The dowager's flare for melodrama tickled Brimble. Not that he had the smallest intention of revealing his amusement. What a blessing he was accustomed to schooling his features to hide his thoughts.

"Ah, well, it is not your fault my son is so unfeeling. Put me in the next best suite available. And tell Twicket to air another bedchamber while she's at it."

"Another chamber, your ladyship?"

"Ain't that what I just said?" she bellowed querulously. "I trust you're not going deaf?"

"I sincerely hope not, my lady," came Brimble's dignified response.

His puzzlement at the dowager's request cleared as he spotted her daughter making her descent from the carriage. Beaming, he said, "Good afternoon, Lady Jane."

"Good day, Brimble. You look fit."

"Indeed, ma'am, I'm in sound health."

"Enough of your blather," burst in the marchioness. "My arthritis is plaguing me something fierce. Give me your arm, Brimble."

"With pleasure, my lady," responded the butler gallantly.

Pity the marquess was in London instead of on hand to defend his bride from the rough side of the dowager's tongue, Brimble mused as he assisted the marchioness up the stone steps and into the manor. Pounds to pennies she resented being usurped by her daughter-in-law and meant to take revenge by making her life a misery. Even so, he dare not lift a finger to help the young lady for fear of being turned off by an enraged dowager — should she succeed in continuing to rule the roost. Besides, it was not his place to interfere with the affairs of the nobility. The younger marchioness would just have to face up to her mother-in-law herself.

Twicket awaited them in the entrance hall, a sly smirk on her countenance that the kindly butler suspected did not bode well for the new mistress, whom the housekeeper appeared to resent. Leaving the dowager in her capable hands, Brimble hurried off to supervise the footmen as they carried in a mountain of luggage from the coach.

Arising from a deep curtsey, the housekeeper said to the marchioness, "Delighted you've come, my lady. And your daughter as well, of course." She turned to Lady Jane. "Your old rooms are being aired, ma'am."

Jane managed a weak smile. "Excellent. Mama, my head is pounding. I believe I'll go on up and lie down."

The dowager, who'd never suffered a headache in her life, glared unsympathetically at her daughter. She was about to issue a scold when she noticed Jane's sickly countenance and relented.

"You do look on the verge of collapse," she blustered. "By all means run along."

As Jane climbed the winding stairs, Twicket pointedly cleared her throat. "My lady, I regret being unable to install you in your former quarters, but his lordship insisted they be given to his bride. I trust you will be comfortable in the Lavender Suite. I've already instructed the chambermaid to prepare it for you — unless you prefer another, of course?"

"Pray don't countermand your orders on

my account. Naturally, I'd prefer my old rooms, but since that pleasure is denied me, it makes no difference where I sleep," boomed the dowager, her homely features set in a childish pout that belied her disclaimer.

"I've taken the liberty of ordering tea served in the drawing-room while you wait for your suite to be readied."

The marchioness brightened perceptibly. "I could do with a dish," she admitted.

Twicket gave a long sigh. "I'd best warn you before I take you there. Brace yourself for a shock. So many changes since your last visit."

"Humph! I collect your new mistress didn't waste a minute putting her stamp on the place. I can only pray her taste is not too vulgar."

"I am not at liberty to venture an opinion. Suffice to say, the young lady and I don't see eye to eye."

The dowager's eyebrows shot up. "I trust her manners are not as hopeless as her breeding."

Twicket sent her a pitying look. "A most regrettable misalliance, my lady. How your heart must ache as a consequence of Master Sebastian's folly."

Unhappily for the housekeeper, in her

zeal to discredit Diantha she unwittingly stepped over an invisible line.

Taking umbrage, the dowager marchioness drew her short buxom body to its full height and said haughtily, "You forget yourself, Twicket. How dare you criticize my son's judgement?"

The housekeeper scrambled to mend her fences. "Indeed, my lady, I beg pardon. It certainly was not my intention to question the actions of my betters."

"No need to grovel, Twicket," the marchioness said gruffly, her pique mollified by the servant's abject apology. "Go about your business!"

"Yes, my lady." The housekeeper dropped a curtsey and backed hastily out of the intimidating noblewoman's presence.

Left to her own devices, the dowager's gaze narrowed pensively. Twicket had an older sister in service in London. More likely than not, that's where she'd gleaned her information in regard to Sebastian's wife's illegitimacy. Pity the servants were such notorious gossips, the dowager thought as she made for the drawing room, her pace as fast as her short, arthritic limbs would allow. Never a good traveller, she was exhausted after rattling along the rutted roads since dawn and required a re-storative to wash away the dust that coated her mouth and throat. And woe to Cook should she not recall her ladyship's favourite blend was Bohea and that she liked it brewed strong. As for the troublesome chit who was now her daughter-in-law, she'd deal with her later.

At the threshold of the drawing-room, her ladyship's jaw dropped. She was never one to let go of her prejudices easily, but the empire sofa, re-covered in a green-and-gold-striped satin, earned a reluctant nod of approval.

Seating herself, she perused the room for further changes. A maid stole in quietly, deposited the silver tea service on a table adjacent to the sofa, and withdrew.

After one sip of the rejuvenating brew — prepared exactly to her taste — the dowager wrapped her fingers around the teacup to allow the warmth radiating from the hot tea to seep into her misshapen knuckles. Arthritis was so . . . crippling, she reflected sadly, then, determined not to dwell on her affliction, firmly directed her thoughts back to the room's dramatic transformation.

She could not help but wonder how she would have fared had her deceased husband given his permission — along with the necessary funds — to redecorate. However, the late marquess would never have agreed to let her spend a single groat on any improvements to his property, his soul ambition in life being to squander his funds at the gaming tables.

Nevertheless, the dowager doubted — even assuming she'd been given free rein — she could have managed such a happy effect. Her brow puckered. For as long as she could remember the window hangings had been a dull burgundy, which had tended to make the room seem dark and gloomy. But now, new draperies tied back with braided cording graced the windows, their colour a rich burnished gold that highlighted the gilt edging of the painted ceiling and picked up the gold accents in the Axminster rug. As a result, the room seemed more spacious, yet, paradoxically, cheerful and cosy.

As she refilled her cup, the dowager conceded the gel's taste was impeccable. Indeed, the marchioness could envision how delightful the room would appear with sunlight streaming through the windows, instead of the light drizzle now falling outside.

Her ladyship was reaching for her third

macaroon when the sound of the harpsichord came into her consciousness. Ears perked, she leaned back into her chair and closed her eyes. Someone had chosen a hauntingly sad melody, one she was not familiar with. Excellent musician, the dowager acknowledged, allowing her thoughts to drift.

The marchioness was aroused from her catnap when the unseen player launched into Beethoven's *Moonlight Sonata*. Egged on by curiosity, she rousted her aching bones off the sofa and, with the enthusiasm of an eager child anticipating a sweet, lumbered from the room.

However, as she neared the music room, her step slowed. Whoever was playing was gifted. It would be a pity if her uninvited presence broke the musician's concentration. Uncertain of whether to advance or retreat, the dowager hesitated.

As a young matron, she'd derived much pleasure from the fine instrument currently being played. Alas, for some years past, due to the insidious advance of arthritis, the harpsichord had remained silent. But now the music she heard was so exquisite that it made her weep. Unable to stand the suspense another second, she cautiously peeked round the threshold.

She beheld a slender, raven-haired young woman whose fingers flew nimbly up and down the keyboard. Deeply moved, the dowager felt all her stubbornly held preconceptions melting away.

She studied the girl for several moments, before the young woman, apparently sensing her scrutiny, glanced towards the entrance and abruptly broke off playing.

So this was Sebastian's wife! In addition to her musical skills, the dowager had to admire the forthright expression in the gel's grey eyes. Perhaps her son's choice wasn't as unsuitable as she'd assumed.

At the sight of the sturdy-looking woman with unmistakable aristocratic bearing, Diantha climbed to her feet.

For a seeming eon, neither woman moved nor spoke. The spell was finally broken by the dowager. "My child, you play so beautifully, it is wicked of me to interrupt."

"Not at all, ma'am." Diantha threw the marchioness a puzzled look. "I can't think what has got into Brimble that he didn't announce you. Are you, perchance, a neighbour?"

"No, my dear, I am your mother-in-law, the Dowager Marchioness of Ravistock."

"Good heavens, I cannot imagine why

the servants have suddenly decided to behave in such a ramshackle fashion. I beg your pardon, ma'am, for not greeting you upon your arrival, but, you see, no one told me."

"Pray don't refine on it," the marchioness begged as she stepped painfully forwards, tears streaming unchecked down her runnelled cheeks. "I'm glad no one saw fit to disturb you. Only think, it might have deprived me of your delightful concert."

"You're very good to say so, ma'am." Diantha's manner was grave. She was disturbed by her mother-in-law's tears, but at a loss as to what to say or do to stem them.

"No such thing. Music is my passion. In fact, in my salad days I used to play myself."

The marchioness gave a watery chuckle. Then, to Diantha's relief, she pulled out a handkerchief tucked in the cuff of her sleeve, dashed away her tears, and wiped her nose.

"How nice we have our love of music in common. But, ma'am, whyever did you give it up?"

Slowly the dowager held out her hands. Eying her gnarled fingers swollen with arthritis, Diantha said, "Oh, what a pity you may no longer play."

"Pish, tish! I've lived with my affliction for so long, I've grown quite resigned to my fate. Thanks be to God there is nothing wrong with my hearing. Since my son has had the good sense to marry such a gifted musician, I collect I may look forward to many impromptu concerts in future."

Diantha gave her mother-in-law a tremulous smile. "Indeed, ma'am, it will be my pleasure."

A week later found Diantha humming a few bars of "Green Sleeves" as she arranged fresh flowers — picked earlier that morning — in a terra-cotta vase. At least, she reflected, with Sebastian gone from home, she could sing to her heart's content. A faint frown disturbed her brow. Since her marriage, it had been hard to remember to curb the impulse, for singing was second nature to her. However, knowing her husband's aversion to amateur songbirds and having no desire to give him a disgust of her, she'd managed to refrain whenever he was within earshot.

Forcing a smile, Diantha snipped the stem of a rose. The fog had finally lifted the day before, raising her spirits, and she was determined not to tumble back into another useless round of self-pity.

Brimble entered, beaming. Amused to see the normally sober-faced butler smile, Diantha asked, "What's put you in such high fettle?"

"My lady, one of the master's servants has arrived from London."

"At last!" came Diantha's spontaneous cry.

"He is waiting outside with a letter for you."

"Pray, send him in, Brimble."

Minutes later, her husband's tiger staggered in carrying a wicker basket on one arm and a half-grown cat struggling to escape from the other.

"Good heavens! Jeremy, is that Caesar?"

Hearing its name, the cat managed to wiggle free from the boy's grasp, but although Diantha rushed forwards to fondle it, her attempt came to naught. Nose in the air, totally ignoring its former mistress, the feline advanced to the hearth and proceeding to preen itself.

"Well!" exclaimed Diantha, visibly nettled.

Jeremy lugged the basket across the room and set it down next to Caesar. Intrigued, Diantha enquired, "What's inside?"

"Mess of kittens, my lady. Present from the guv'ner."

"Kittens?" Diantha sailed to the hearth and lifted the lid. Discovering five pair of luminous blue eyes staring up at her, she exclaimed, "Oh, you darlings!"

But, after fondling them for a few moments, she closed the lid. "Strays, I presume?"

Jeremy shot her a pitying look. "No, my lady. They be Caesar's litter. You see, 'e ain't a 'im, 'e's a 'er."

The instant the words registered, Diantha laughed, then, recovering from her amused surprise, shifted her gaze to the lad. Noting his grin, she awarded him a sweet smile. "Thank you for escorting Caesar and *her* family from London. Do you mean to stay or return to town?"

"The guv needs me with 'im in Lunndon. Me and the coachman 'ave orders to return at once."

"I see. Pray thank his lordship for his, er . . . unusual present. And if I don't see you again, have a pleasant journey."

Though dismissed, the tiger stubbornly held his ground.

"Was there something else, Jeremy?"

"Aye. Kittens ain't all 'e sent you, my lady. The 'ousekeeper took charge of the

202

ells of cloth I brang, and the guv gave me this 'ere letter and bade me deliver it into your 'and." As he spoke, he drew it from a shirt pocket and presented it to her.

Gracious! Brimble had mentioned a letter. How could she have forgotten?

"Brimble can direct you to the kitchen. Tell Cook I said to feed you."

"Ay, my lady. Thank you."

As the lad sauntered from the room, Caesar rose and trailed after him, her tail up, her nose high.

Diantha giggled. What kind of a mother blithely deserted her offspring? She'd heard cats were independent, but Caesar's attitude was outside of enough!

Her countenance sobered as she examined the sealed missive in her hand. It was approaching a month since Sebastian had left. She'd much prefer his presence to a letter, but at least he'd finally written. Breaking the seal, she scanned the contents.

My dearest, Diantha,

I am sorry to say the rebellion in Spain has catapulted the Admiralty into a fever of activity. My presence is needed here for at least another two weeks. I enclose several ells of blue brocade that Ellsworth, my private secretary, found at Harding, Howell & Co. I trust the basket of kittens makes you smile. Patience, my sweet. I, too, am exceedingly vexed by the delay. Pray God we may be reunited soon. Until then, I remain your devoted husband.

Sebastian's signature was scrawled at the bottom of the sheet of parchment.

Scanning it a second time, Diantha experienced a wave of tenderness. With a deep sigh, she refolded the letter in thirds and slipped it into her pocket.

Was it possible Sebastian did love her despite his long absence? she wondered. Frankly, she missed him so very much. Without him, pursuits she'd formerly taken pleasure in seemed flat.

She frowned. Gifts were nice, but the fact remained that her husband was still in London while she was in Wiltshire. Furthermore, since he obviously had no idea when he might return to the Ravistock country seat, she had every reason to expect an invitation to join him in town. Alas, no such invitation had been issued. The painful truth was that he didn't want her with him. Mayhap, he hadn't missed her at all.

★ ★ ★

A month after her mother-in-law's arrival, Diantha resolutely pinned a smile on her face and entered the drawingroom.

"Here she is at last, Jane," the dowager marchioness proclaimed in a stentorian voice that never failed to rattle the china.

"Indeed, ma'am, I beg your pardon for my tardiness," Diantha responded. "When Charity asked me to help her distribute hand-me-downs to the poor, I had no idea it would take an entire afternoon."

"Charity?" quizzed the dowager.

"Reverend Chase's wife, Mama," Lady Jane interjected.

"Yes, of course. Don't fret, child," the marchioness advised. "As you were involved in performing your Christian duty, it scarcely signifies."

The dowager gazed at the lovely young woman who'd married her eldest son. To be candid, his continued absence vexed her. Particularly as he'd now lingered in town for the better part of two months. Furthermore, her bosom bow in Bath, Lady Dalrymple, whose niece had just returned from her first Season in town, had written to say that Lady Fitzwilliam continued to make a cake of herself. Even more disturbing, the dowager's friend had intimated that Sebastian may have taken her up again. If true, the marchioness was deeply sorry for it. Diantha was a sweet child and didn't deserve such callous indifference.

The dowager compressed her lips in a rigid line. Naturally, she wouldn't dream of breathing a word of these disturbing rumours to her daughter-in-law, but just the same, Sebastian must be brought to his senses before he tossed away all chance of future marital harmony.

Though patience was not her long suit, her ladyship forced herself to bide her time until Diantha had taken a few fortifying sips of tea and had selected a macaroon from the tray then asked Jane to fetch her cashmere shawl.

"There's something I wish to discuss with you," the marchioness said.

"Indeed. What is it?" asked Diantha.

"Summer's on the wane. I must return to Bath."

"Oh, dear. Must you?"

"There's more. Harry and Will must come also. The boys are all out at the elbows and must see a tailor before they return to Cambridge for the Michaelmas term."

The news depressed Diantha. She'd be

all alone at the manor, with the exception of the servants, of course. If only Sebastian would come home. She longed to share small everyday pleasures with him. She'd made progress on horseback and longed to catch the warm approval in his eyes. More than that, she longed for his comforting presence beside her — especially during the seemingly interminable nights.

"My dear child, you've gone quite pale. Shall I ring for a vinaigrette?"

The dowager's robust voice seemed to come from the far end of a lengthy tunnel. This would never do! Sternly, Diantha called herself to order.

"No need, ma'am. It is just that I shall miss all of you most dreadfully."

"Exactly what I wish to discuss. I swear I am all out of patience with Sebastian. Why pine away here waiting for him to show up? Accompany me to Bath for a visit instead."

"Go with you to Bath?" A spark of light shone in Diantha's eyes but was swiftly extinguished. "It's kind of you to invite me, but Sebastian expects to find me here when he returns."

"Pish, tish! Listen to me, gel. If you continue to behave like a meek little lamb, that inattentive son of mine will continue to be inconsiderate. For pity's sake, show some backbone!"

Much struck by the force of her mother-in-law's argument, Diantha's nerves were in such a state she felt torn between laughter and tears. A change of scene might be just the ticket to distract her from her loneliness. Why not go? After all, why should Sebastian object?

Chapter 12

In Hanover Square, Sebastian slept hunched over at his desk, his head nestled in a stack of Admiralty papers. A firm, masculine hand tugged on his shoulder. He tried to shrug it off, but the manly grasp proved tenacious.

"Wake up, Ravistock. It's morning."

Groggy from sleep, Sebastian slowly raised his head to peer bleary-eyed at his tormentor.

"Ellsworth? What the deuce?"

"Bloody fool! Fell asleep over your work again."

The marquess grinned sheepishly. Although Ellsworth was at present his private secretary, they'd known each other as boys. Jack had never been one to mince words.

"You wouldn't be so crabby if you'd slept in a bed once in a while instead of sprawled at your desk."

In the vain hope of alleviating a crick in his neck, Sebastian gingerly rotated his head. "Sleep be damned! I've been stuck in town for ages! I'll make do with catnaps if it means I can wade through these curst papers. I'm determined to leave at the end of the month."

"You can't. Not with all the work that remains."

Sebastian eyed the stack of papers on his desk. Jack was right of course. His shoulders slumped.

"Believe me, old chap, I sympathise, but your bride won't be best pleased if you ruin your health."

"Fustian! I've the constitution of a plough horse!"

Eager to prove his point, Sebastian tried to stand. Alas, both legs were asleep and refused to support him. His powerful frame tottered backward into his chair.

"By God, I'm timber-toed!"

"Legs lack feeling, do they? I'm not surprised. Here, take my arm."

"Damn you, Jack, stop treating me as if I were your grandmama!"

Ellsworth grinned. "As you wish."

When the prickly sensations in his lower limbs eased, Sebastian rose. "Excuse me. I must bathe and dress. I've a meeting to attend at Whitehall."

Upon her arrival in Bath, Diantha's

spirits perked up. From her mother-in-law's house in Laura Place, it was but a comfortable walk up Great Pulteney Street to Sydney Gardens. Harry and Will escorted her there once she'd settled in.

"At night there are capital illuminations and fireworks," Harry volunteered.

"And concerts," Will added.

Exploring the grounds, Diantha discovered Sydney Gardens was hexagonal in shape and boasted a wide variety of flowers. However, it was its Labyrinth that intrigued her.

"Never saw a girl who enjoyed getting lost as much as you do," Harry had teased the fourth time he led her from the maze.

The next day, Diantha set out with her sister-in-law, whom she'd come to regard as a dear friend. In Milsom Street, she saw a hat she admired in a shop window.

"Do look, Jane. Is that not the prettiest concoction?"

"Which one?"

"Why the one with the coquelicot ribbons."

"Very fetching. Do you wish to go inside?"

Diantha hesitated. "I suppose it's very dear."

"Costs naught to try it on."

"Very true!" She linked her arm with Jane's. "By all means, let's have a closer look."

After purchasing the hat and exchanging their books at Duffield's, they strolled into the Pump Room. Here, they met the dowager marchioness, fresh from her daily dip in one of the resort's heated mineral baths which seemed to have a salutatory effect on her arthritis.

"La, child, I've entered your name in the subscription book. Mr. King looks forward to meeting you."

"Mr. King?" Diantha asked.

The dowager marchioness nodded. "Take care not to offend him when he calls. He's the Master of Ceremonies of the Upper Assembly Room."

Diantha wrinkled her brow. She did not perfectly understand why keeping herself in Mr. King's good graces was of paramount importance. But, before she had a chance to delve into the matter, Jane said, "Do look, Mama! Lady Dalrymple's signalling you."

"So she is! And her niece is with her. Shall we join them?"

Necessary introductions dealt with, Lady Dalrymple smiled at the dowager. "I plan to host a small dinner party on Thursday. I hope you and your new daughter-in-law will contrive to come. Lady Jane, too, of course, if she cares to grace us with her presence."

"You are too kind," Jane responded. "However, I prefer my own hearth."

The dowager chortled. "The truth with no bark on it is Jane don't shine in Society. As to Diantha and myself, I'll have to let you know. Our plans are a bit unsettled."

"I hope both of you will attend. Your daughter-in-law and my niece are of an age. I am persuaded they are destined to become bosom bows. I daresay after London, Bath seems a trifle flat to Alison."

"La, Auntie, you are so droll." Miss Stanley gave an affected titter. "True, Bath has little variety. However, after my gay whirl in town, I declare I'm worn to a thread and could do with a bit of rustication."

Bosom bows? All my eye and Betty Martin! Diantha silently vowed. She resolved to remain aloof from the vapid young woman, having gotten her fill of spoiled aristocratic beauties the year she'd taught music at the Seminary.

Strolling homeward beside her mother-in-law's sedan chair, Diantha's curiosity got the better of her. "Jane, do you never go out in society?"

"Certainly, I do. I am fond of music so I attend concerts. What I avoid are activities I dislike."

"Lady Dalrymple's dinner party, for example?"

Jane laughed. "Most definitely! Since I consider her ladyship a dreadful bore and her niece a spiteful cat, I turn down all her invitations."

"But, spending evenings by yourself, don't you get lonely?"

Jane shook her head. "Believe me, after being run off my feet all day by dearest Mama whenever her aching joints make her peevish, I relish my solitude."

Her sister-in-law was full of surprises. Before coming to know her better, Diantha had considered Jane to be . . . spineless. However, as time passed, fresh insight had prompted her to revise her opinion. Granted Jane lacked the gumption to confront her mother head-on, but even Diantha, who wasn't easily cowed, would hesitate to do that. With the exception of the formidable dowager, perhaps it would be more accurate to describe Jane as reticent, rather than overly timid.

Wearing an emerald green gown with a daringly, low-cut neckline, Lady Fitzwilliam smiled coolly as her butler ushered the marquess into the blue drawing room.

"La, Sebastian, so you've decided to visit me after all. Shall I ring for tea or do you prefer something stronger?"

Ravistock gave a bark of laughter. "Something stronger, by all means."

To be candid, he was so angry he felt on the verge of exploding, but somehow he managed to hold his tongue while the dignified butler poured him a glass of sherry.

"That will be all, Biggers," said Lady Fitzwilliam.

She waited until her majordomo withdrew before awarding Sebastian a conspiratorial wink.

"Now we may be cosy." She patted the seat beside her. "Come, darling, sit here. It's like old times, don't you agree?"

"Cut line, Honoria. Well you know I'm here in response to your note. Madam, if you think to lure me back to your bed by threatening suicide, you've mistaken your man."

A look of uncertainty flickered briefly in my lady's green eyes. But, almost immediately, she recovered her aplomb. "Gammon! It is not as if your marriage is a love match. If that were the case, you'd have brought your wife to London, instead of leaving her buried in the country."

Sebastian struggled to hang on to his temper. The truth was he missed Diantha terribly and regretted leaving her behind. He'd never dreamt he'd be tied up this long with naval affairs. Every time he thought he would be able to return to her, another urgent matter came up. Now, after such a long delay, he was afraid that if he simply summoned her to town she would be resentful. However, he'd be damned if he'd bare his soul to his former mistress. His innermost feelings were none of her business.

"Madam, I meant what I said. Our affair is over."

Honoria's pretty face crumpled. "After all we meant to each other? How can you be so cruel?"

Ravistock gave a weary sigh. "I've no wish to hurt you, Lady Fitzwilliam."

"Do you not?" Arising, she touched his sleeve, and when he peered at her quizzically, she fluttered her eyelashes and said, "Surely, you are funning. What harm will it do if you dally with one of your most . . . intimate friends?"

Sebastian shook off her hand as if it were a coiled serpent. "Madam, you forget yourself! I've no wish to resume our affair. If you will have the truth, I have too much regard for my wife to dishonour her."

Lady Fitzwilliam seethed with rage. "What! You choose that baseborn chit over me? That's an insult. Mark my words, I'll make you sorry."

"Threats, Honoria?" he enquired silkily.

Her ladyship's face set in a mulish pout. "All my plans are in shambles, thanks to your fickle heart."

Ravistock raised an eyebrow. "Doing it up too brown, my dear. I never led you to expect more than a brief fling."

"Oh, Sebastian, how can you say so? I'd hoped to become your marchioness."

The marquess looked amazed. "My marchioness? Have you taken leave of your senses?"

Honoria appeared stung. "Of course I have not! I had such plans. Once we'd eloped, Henry would have been obliged to divorce me, freeing us to marry. It was a famous scheme. And now it lies in ruins," she wailed. "T— Thanks to that . . . that creature you married instead of me."

"Have a care, madam, you are speaking

of the woman I love!"

"You love her? It's not to be borne! So help me, I'll get even with you for this."

"Will you, vixen?" He awarded her an insouciant shrug. "I give you leave to do your damnedest."

His hand was on the doorknob when Honoria cried, "Sebastian, wait!"

He spun around. What now? he thought. She rushed forward, faltering as she drew near. "Couldn't we . . . ?"

"No, we could not!"

"Very well, then, I will have my revenge." Honoria's green eyes took on a hard shine. "I shall tell Sir Henry you cuckolded him. If I know my husband, he'll fly into a rage and call you out."

Sebastian struggled to speak evenly. "Honoria, Henry isn't up to my weight. Such a course would be most unwise."

Lady Fitzwilliam gave a scornful laugh. "Ha! Don't think to fob me off with such taradiddle!"

"Clearly, I am wasting my time trying to reason with a bedlamite. Madam, I bid you good day."

"I hope he kills you," Honoria screeched as he crossed the threshold.

Though he heard her, he did not check his stride. In the entrance hall he found

Biggers waiting with his hat and cane. The butler's face remained impassive, though Ravistock was almost certain he'd overheard them airing their differences. How could he not, with her ladyship shouting like a fishmonger? At least, Biggers could be counted on to hold his tongue. Not so the rest of the staff. No doubt the bare bones of their quarrel would travel like a flash fire from servant to servant until all of Mayfair was privy to the latest juicy tale.

Sebastian climbed into his phaeton and took up the reins, filled with remorse. He could only pray that none of this came to his wife's ears. He couldn't bear to see her hurt. Would that he'd never dallied with Honoria. But it was far too late for regrets. By his own folly, he'd come to this pass.

The evening of the dinner party at Lady Dalrymple's, Diantha took great care with her toilet. In deference to her state of half mourning, she selected a round dress of lavender crepe, spotted with white satin and worn over a white sarcenet slip. The gown was one of many ordered by Sebastian from Madam Lavelle, and knowing she was dressed in the first stare of fashion lent Diantha confidence. Even so, gazing at her reflection while Katie wove white flowers intermixed with pearls through her raven locks, she felt a twinge of regret. How she wished that Sebastian could be on hand to accompany her the first time she ventured out into Society since their marriage.

At the foot of the stairs, Diantha found her mother-in-law waiting. "La, child, I am persuaded you will cast all the other females in the shade."

"It is a beautiful gown, is it not?"

"My dear, it's top of the trees!"

In companionable accord, they rode up Great Pulteney Street to No. 4 Sydney Place in a closed carriage. Inside the mansion, Lady Dalrymple greeted her friend.

"My dear, Mathilda, I knew you wouldn't fail me," she gushed. "But come, let us repair to the drawing room."

"Penny for your thoughts, my lady."

Diantha gazed up at a tall blond Adonis with a devil-may-care grin. Prudently lowering her lashes to hide the flicker of amusement in her eyes, she said coolly, "I beg your pardon, sir. Have we been introduced?"

To her annoyance, his grin widened. "A high stickler I vow! Excuse me, my sweet, while I rectify my oversight."

Diantha stared after him, then with a

shrug decided to dismiss the brash young fribble from her mind. However, her intention was rendered unworkable by the tenacity of that gentleman, who now returned with their hostess in tow.

Lady Dalrymple beamed first at Diantha and then at her handsome escort. "Arthur, you rogue, I must commend your taste. My lady is as pretty as she can stare."

"Agreed, but more the point, who is she?"

Her ladyship's eyes twinkled with amusement. "Diantha, may I present Mr. Rutherford. Arthur, this is Lady Ravistock."

His jaw dropped. "Ravistock's bride? Well, I'll be. . . ."

To see the arrogant young gentleman thwarted in his single-minded attempt to fix her interest seemed just in Diantha's eyes. Thus, when Rutherford had the temerity to add, "So this is the minx who manoeuvred the elusive marquess into the parson's mousetrap," she was understandably vexed.

"Naughty boy!" Lady Dalrymple scolded playfully. "You owe the marchioness an apology."

Eyes flashing, Diantha said icily, "Indeed, sir, your manners are deplorable."

Thoroughly chastened, he sobered. "You are quite right to ring a peal over me. If my thoughtless teasing caused you a single moment's distress, I am heartily sorry for it."

"Handsomely said, Arthur, handsomely said."

The dinner gong sounded. Initially, all was confusion as each gentleman present sought the lady they were to lead into the dining room.

Seated midtable, Diantha was appalled to discover that Mr. Rutherford had been assigned the chair to her left. Having delivered him a setdown, she'd intended to avoid any further contact with the flirtatious young man. Unhappily, for her proper table etiquette demanded she converse with each dinner partner in turn.

Happy to postpone the inevitable until her hostess turned table, Diantha struck up a conversation with the gentleman on her right. Alas, that florid-faced peer proved to be a disgruntled Whig, who proved on and on in regard to the deprivation suffered by the poor as a result of the Corn Laws. Though she sympathised with the plight of the needy, his mention of starving children put paid to her appetite. Consequently, she could not help feeling a trifle cross when she saw that the Whig did not share her sudden aversion for food, but, instead, availed himself of each dish offered.

A quarter of an hour later it was almost a relief to turn to speak with Mr. Rutherford. However, before she had a chance to say a word, Miss Stanley addressed a remark to him from across the table, seemingly oblivious to the fact that Society's high sticklers considered such a practice a breach of good manners.

Diantha readily conceded Miss Stanley looked all the crack in a mint green gown, her wheat blonde hair dressed high. Nonetheless, she felt the smug look on the incomparable's face detracted from her beauty. At first, Diantha could not fathom why Miss Stanley considered her a rival. At length, she concluded that, since the three of them were the only young people present, Miss Stanley resented Mr. Rutherford's lighthearted flirtation with Diantha. Indeed, catching the possessive gleam in the young woman's eye whenever she glanced at Mr. Rutherford, it was obvious she'd set her cap for the handsome young blade.

Determined not to be accused of poaching on the beauty's preserves,

Diantha decided to treat that gentleman as coolly as she could — without being unpardonably rude.

Lady Dalrymple stood and led the procession of ladies into the drawing room. There, Miss Stanley wandered from group to group, never lingering long in any one spot. Finally her aunt exclaimed, "For heaven's sake, Alison, stop flitting from pillar to post. Why not entertain us with your latest piece on the pianoforte?"

Miss Stanley moved with such alacrity towards that instrument, Diantha suspected she'd hoped her aunt would ask her to play. Yet, to Diantha's trained ear she proved to be an indifferent musician at best. When the beauty hit a sour note, Diantha managed to disguise her wince by quickly raising her fan. Shortly thereafter, the men joined them. Instantly, Miss Stanley rose from the piano stool and prettily begged the gentlemen to be seated.

"We are in for a treat," she announced. "My aunt informs me, that not only does Lady Ravistock play, she also sings. I am persuaded with only a little coaxing, she'll consent to entertain us."

She wants to embarrass me, Diantha thought. Well, she'll catch cold at that! She almost laughed in the beauty's gloating face as she passed her on the way to the pianoforte. Seating herself, Diantha ran her fingers over the keyboard before launching into an excerpt from Haydn's *Toy Symphony*. Afterwards, she played a favored portion from Mozart's *Marriage of Figaro*.

When the last note faded, a hush fell. Just as Diantha began to wonder if the audience would have preferred lighter fare, the clapping started. Rising, she acknowledged their kudos with a modest bob of her head. Indeed, she would have deserted the pianoforte altogether, but for the clamour of voices begging her to sing.

"Very well," she said, bowing to the inevitable.

In her rich, husky contralto, she regaled them with several English folk songs, ending with "Green Sleeves." Having learned her lesson, she did not linger at the pianoforte until the applause died. Instead, she retreated to a wing chair in an inconspicuous corner. It was from this vantage point that she saw Miss Stanley advancing toward her. As she neared, the air prickled with animosity. Obviously, Diantha's successful performance had put the vindictive beauty's nose further out of joint.

"Mind if I join you for a nonce, my lady?"

"By all means do."

Taking an opposing chair, Miss Stanley beamed. "Bath is such a backwater spot. One misses the hurly-burly pace of constant *ton* parties one finds in London." The beauty's bright smile was overshadowed by the malicious gleam in her eyes. "Not to mention the up-to-the-minute gossip. Shall I bring you up-to-date?"

Diantha stood. "Save your breath, Miss Stanley. I've an aversion to it."

Cool smile still intact, the incomparable cocked her head to one side. "Very commendable to be sure. Just the same, as it concerns your husband, I thought possibly. . . ."

Diantha's stomach lurched. She felt torn by conflicting emotions. On one hand, she wanted to rush from the suddenly cloying atmosphere of the fashionable drawing room. On the other, she recognized she'd know no peace unless she heard her tormenter out. Weakkneed, she sank back into the chair.

"Pray continue, Miss Stanley."

"Very well. The vulgar spectacle Lady Fitzwilliam and your husband made of themselves by clinging so scandalously whilst waltzing at the Leicester ball is the latest *on-dit*."

Miss Stanley had the gall to flash her a cat's-in-the-creampot smile. Diantha longed to slap that odious smirk off the beauty's face. Instead, she kept her hands firmly clasped in her lap.

Sebastian, how could you so dishonour me? Diantha silently grieved. Fortunately, despite her anguish, she had the presence of mind to keep her countenance blank. Not for the world would she allow this . . . this . . . tattlemonger the satisfaction of knowing how deeply she'd wounded her.

"What you prattle is mere idle conjecture," Diantha stated quietly.

Miss Stanley's eyes glittered with malicious glee. "It is said, the wife is always the last to know. If you prefer to keep your head buried in the sand, that's entirely up to you." Having spent all her venom, the beauty climbed to her feet. "Excuse me. The tea tray has arrived, and I promised my aunt I'd pour."

Heartbroken, Diantha lingered in her self-imposed seclusion. Fool that she was, she'd swallowed all Sebastian's excuses while he'd dallied in London with his paramour. Oh, God, the hurt was so deep, it seared to the very core of her soul.

"My dear child, whatever are you doing hiding way in a corner?"

Diantha blinked her mother-in-law into focus. "I was . . . thinking."

"Were you, puss? In that case, here's food for thought. Lady Dalrymple's guests are so taken with your lovely voice that several have expressed the hope you might agree to sing a solo from one of Handel's oratorios at the Octagon Chapel of a Sunday."

"Indeed, ma'am, is such an undertaking considered respectable?"

"Eminently so, my dear. Elizabeth Linley sang there before she wed Sheridan. As did Caroline Herschel, under her brother's direction, until Sir William switched his interest to the discovery of comets."

"In that case, I'd be delighted."

The dowager's homely face took on a pensive cast. "It is a mere formality of course, but I'll write Sebastian and request his permission, though I cannot imagine why he'd object."

Preoccupied, Diantha scarcely heard. To think she'd worried that Sebastian might be annoyed with her for not waiting for him at Teale Manor. Sadly, he'd all but forgotten her existence. Furthermore, his work at the Admiralty was a mere sham. Never again would she be so trusting!

Chapter 13

Sebastian was working at his desk when Parker, his high-in-the-instep butler, entered the library bearing a letter on a salver.

"From my wife?"

"No, milord. From the dowager marchioness."

"Oh."

After dismissing Parker, Sebastian glared at his mother's missive. Not that he was annoyed with her. Rather, his irritation stemmed from the sharp stab of disappointment he'd felt when told the letter wasn't from Diantha.

Sebastian frowned. Not that he had any right to expect one. He was a terrible correspondent himself. He'd wanted to send her love letters but had been too embarrassed. All he'd been able to manage was an occasional terse note.

Arising, he linked his hands behind him and paced back and forth across the carpet. God, but he missed her. How he longed to toss aside his responsibilities and rush to her side. However, his conscience wouldn't let him leave his superiors in the lurch. Not now that Portugal was also embroiled in a rebellion every bit as serious as the turmoil in Spain.

Even now he could invite Diantha to join him, but that seemed selfish. Not only was the city sweltering in an unprecedented heat wave, but the long hours he must devote to mobilizing the British Fleet ensured he'd have little time to spend with her.

No question his lady wife was better off in Wiltshire. Honoria's brazen conduct at the Leicester ball was only now beginning to be superceded by talk of Queen Caroline's trial, scheduled to begin in a fortnight. The ugly gossip still circulating would be sure to hurt someone as naive as Diantha. And Sebastian refused to cause her an instant's pain if it could be avoided.

There was also Honoria's threat to exact revenge to consider. If she told Sir Henry he'd been cuckolded — hothead that he was — he'd be sure to issue a challenge. However, since four days had passed since Sebastian had called on Honoria, he was hopeful — once her temper cooled — she'd had a change of heart.

Sebastian knit his brow. Equally vexing, if he didn't complete his work at the Admiralty soon, he'd lose his chance to make a flying trip to Teale Manor to reassure his bride of his love before the queen's trial began in the House of Lords. Attendance for all able-bodied peers was compulsory. Unfortunately, no one had any idea how long the trial would last. Never in his life had he felt so frustrated as he plucked the letter off his desk and broke its seal.

Skimming the first few lines, he had to grin. By God, here was a switch! Only a few months past, his mother had turned up her nose at the mere suggestion she house Lord Devonwych's daughter. Now, here was Mama writing to confess she'd grown prodigiously fond of Diantha. Such an about-face would be hard to credit, unless one were intimately acquainted with the taking minx who was now his wife.

Reading a little farther, he noted dearest Mama had carried his bride off to Bath for a visit. Splendid! No doubt, Diantha was beginning to grow bored at Teale Manor without him.

However, the scanning of the next few lines wiped the wry grin off his face. The letter shook in his hand as he perused the disturbing portion again in the hope he'd misread it. Unhappily, he had not.

God almighty! How dare Mama undermine his carefully laid groundwork discouraging Diantha from singing! In high dudgeon, the marquess tossed the missive on the desktop and commenced roving the room like a jungle cat trapped in a cage.

He was flabbergasted by his mother's suggestion that he allow his wife to sing a solo from Handel at Bath's famed Octagon Chapel. Sunday service or no, he must absolutely forbid Diantha to sing a note! Were he so irresponsible as to permit her to sing, her debut would be sure to rake up the old scandal. Should that happen, the entire family would end up in the basket.

More important, Sebastian couldn't bear to think how hurt Diantha would be, should she discover the true circumstances of her mother's death. If he had anything to say about it, she never would!

By damn, come hell or high water, he resolved to wind up his affairs at Whitehall by the end of the week. Meantime, he'd write to his mother and forbid her to go ahead with her crackbrained scheme. While he was at it, he'd dash off a brief note to Diantha denying her permission as well.

His gaze narrowed as he dipped his quill

into the inkwell. Knowing Mama, his letter would serve only as a temporary check. Sebastian gave a grim chuckle. Well he knew dearest Mama's stubborn streak! It was imperative he post down to Bath the instant he was free.

Diantha sat in a high-backed wing chair, angled to face the window that overlooked the square. The August day was hot and humid. The overcast sky seemed attuned to her glum frame of mind. Diantha yawned. Since Sebastian's note had come, she'd scarcely slept a wink.

In her hand, she clutched her husband's terse missive. In the past week, she'd read it so many times that the sheet was dog-eared. And each time she did, she sighed. It was mean spirited of Sebastian to forbid her to sing at Octagon Chapel. Singing was as natural as breathing to her. Why didn't he understand that?

Dejected, she peered out at the passing traffic. Her eyelids grew heavy. She dozed.

Some time later, she woke to the sound of male voices engaged in a brangle. Sleepy-eyed, she reluctantly tuned in to Will's heated protest.

"A cart race?" he scoffed. "Harry, of all

the corkbrained ideas, this one takes the palm!"

"Stuff! It will be a splendid lark. Anyhow, even supposing I wished to, I can't back out," Harry confessed, ruefully. "I'm in too deep."

"That's what comes of giving overgenerous odds. Mutton headed to wager when you're bosky."

"Wasn't drunk — only a trifle disguised."

"Never mind splitting hairs, Harry. Any tradesman worth his salt wants an early start. They won't take kindly to us er . . . borrowing their carts for our race."

"So we'll rendezvous at midnight. That'll allow us plenty of time to return the carts before they're missed. Satisfied?"

Will sighed. "I suppose. Say a prayer they don't catch us either taking or returning their property. If they do, it'll be the devil to pay!"

"Curst wet blanket is what you are, Will."

"Leastways I ain't a sapskull like you."

"Oh, for heaven's sake!" Diantha exclaimed as she sprang to her feet. "Stop trading insults and tell me about the cart race."

Harry stared at her, dumbfounded. "Di,

what are you doing here?"

"I *was* sleeping in the wing chair by the window until you woke me."

"My apologies." Her brother-in-law's eyes narrowed in cunning calculation. "Why not toddle off to your bed, where you may rest undisturbed?"

Diantha burst out laughing. "Eager to get rid of me, are you? Too bad. My catnap refreshed me. Now, what about this cart race?"

Harry's brow furrowed. "Look here, Di. A lot of blunt's riding on tonight's race. Want your word you'll keep mum."

"Why certainly, Harry. Happy to oblige, provided . . ."

"Provided?" he prompted warily.

"Provided you take me with you."

"Out of the question!" he snapped.

"All we need is a female along to turn the proceedings into a three-ring circus," Will added.

"Nonsense! I promise not to give you a minute's trouble."

Harry shook his head. "Di, I cannot allow it. Sebastian'd skin me alive."

"Fustian! He has no say over me."

"Don't be daft. He's your husband."

Diantha saw red. The fact that his marriage vows had not stopped Sebastian from resuming his affair with Honoria cut to the bone. Imagine him having the nerve to order her not to sing at the Octagon Chapel! Well, she'd show him.

"Don't be a spoilsport, Harry," she cajoled. "I'll wear breeches and tuck my hair up under a cap. Sebastian's in London. He need never know."

"Even so, I cannot let you come. A marchioness cutting up larks ain't all the thing."

A wave of resentment washed over her. Much she cared if her conduct sank her beyond the pale. She'd tried so hard to leave the schoolroom behind her — to become an exemplary wife Sebastian could be proud of. But did he care? No, he did not! Diantha's voice took on a sharp edge. "Give over, Harry, else I'll blow the gaff."

Both youths stared at her unhappily for several seconds before Harry showed signs of wavering.

"Don't be a fool," Will warned him. "You dare not let her come. Too risky by far. Cancel the race instead."

Harry sighed. "I'd like nothing better, Will, but I've got too much blunt riding on the outcome."

"Then you'll let me tag along?" Diantha asked.

"I suppose. Mind you, if this caper comes to Sebastian's ears, all three of us will be in the suds."

Diantha smiled. "I've said it before, but it bears repeating. Harry, you're a trump."

"Curst loose screw, more like," Will grumbled.

"Stubble it, old chap!" Harry recommended. "When I want your opinion, I'll ask."

At Hanover Square, Sebastian signed the last page of the lengthy document.

"There now," said his solicitor. "Once your two witnesses sign, I'll be on my way back to the city."

Sebastian glanced at his private secretary, who looked hesitant. "You heard the man, Jack. Hop to it."

After Ellsworth signed, Sebastian gave Parker, who appeared equally reluctant, a stern nod. So prodded, the butler stepped forward and painstakingly wrote out his name.

The solicitor blotted the ink dry, rolled up the document and slipped it into an inside coat pocket. "There. It's done all right and tight, your lordship."

"Quite. Parker will see you out."

Sebastian waited until the solicitor departed before quizzing his friend. "Why the long face, Jack?"

"You need to ask? Witnessing your last will and testament is not a task to send me into transports."

"Nor I, old stick. However, since I suspect that the purpose of the meeting Sir Henry has requested is to issue a challenge, prudence dictates I put my affairs in order."

"Probably foxed when he wrote," Ellsworth muttered. "If he were serious, he'd have followed the code and asked you to name your seconds."

From the threshold, the butler interrupted. "My lord, Sir Henry has arrived."

"Give us a few minutes, Parker."

"Very good, milord." Bowing, he departed.

Ravistock lifted a sheath of papers off his desktop which he wrapped in sheepskin and handed to Ellsworth. "Be a good fellow, and deliver this to the Admiralty."

"Your final report I take it?"

Sebastian managed a rueful smile. "How well you know me. I dislike loose ends."

"Just so. I'll scoot round to Whitehall the minute Sir Henry leaves."

"Jack, I don't require a wet nurse. Run it over now. There's a good fellow."

"Well, if you're certain . . ."

"I am. Take yourself off and on your way out tell Parker to show Fitzwilliam up."

Alone with his thoughts, Sebastian felt it ironic that now that his services were no longer in demand at the Admiralty — but for Honoria — he'd be well on his way to Bath. How he chafed at the delay in rejoining Diantha.

Far more disturbing, should Sir Henry call him out, he might die without ever setting eyes on his darling again. Gloomy thought that, he conceded, giving himself a firm shake.

"Sir Henry, my lord," Parker announced.

Fitzwilliam entered the library with a determined expression on his face. Sebastian offered him Madeira or brandy. His visitor firmly declined both, though he did deign to sit when invited to do so.

Civilities satisfied, Sebastian settled into a chair and asked, "How may I serve you, sir?"

"I'm here in regard to my wife."

"I assumed as much. You demand satisfaction?"

"Of a certainty!"

Sebastian sighed. "I'd hoped we might discuss this like rational beings, but naturally I accept your challenge."

"Challenge? Er, . . . not necessarily."

"Explain yourself, sir?"

"To own the truth, Ravistock, I'm not certain a duel will answer."

"Then why the devil have you come?"

"Thought a man-to-man talk might clear the air."

"Talk? No offense, but you're known to be a fire eater."

"Only when foxed. Today I'm sober."

"So you are," Sebastian agreed, after subjecting his guest to a searching look. "Definitely an improvement."

"Oh, I don't want for sense when my wits ain't addled with blue ruin. But let's get to the nub of the matter, shall we?"

"By all means carry on."

"To be candid, I've let Honoria call the tune far too often. She's such a dainty little dish, I misliked the idea of riding rough-shod over her, ya' see? But, of late, I've been, er . . . cogitating. Appears to me, by always giving in to her whims, I lost her respect. Another thing. Instead of calling her to book whenever I saw she was sailing too close to the line, I drank until I was pot valiant. Bad judgement on my part."

Sebastian tugged on his neck-cloth, which suddenly felt too constricting. Listening to Sir Henry bare his soul was exceedingly uncomfortable. However, he could hardly order him to stop after granting him permission to speak.

"But now that I've sworn off spirits, I see things more clearly. When in my cups, I let Honoria goad me into issuing a challenge. But never again. I've put my foot down."

"Good for you, sir! However, before we close this ignoble chapter in which I am persuaded none of us behaved as we ought, I wish to apologize for my part in this sorry affair."

"Apology accepted!" Sir Henry rose. "Shall we shake on it?"

Sebastian firmly clasped the outstretched hand. "Pardon my curiosity, but how is Honoria taking your new stance?"

Fitzwilliam's serious demeanor was lightened by a rueful smile. "She's furious of course. But no matter. I've ordered her to be packed by dawn — else I'll drag her off in the clothes she stands in."

An appreciative gleam kindled in Sebastian's eyes. "I don't imagine that sat too well."

"Of a certainty! Nor did the fact that I'm banishing her to my Irish estate until she learns to be more biddable."

"Good God! I make no doubt she's up in the boughs."

"That she is. However, I'm confident in time we'll come about. Now, my lord, I must bid you good day. I've a welter of details to see to before we leave town."

"Then you'll accompany Lady Fitzwilliam?"

"Yes. I daresay a bout of rustication won't harm me either. I'm thankful to be a baronet and not obliged to remain in London. I suppose you're staying until the trial."

Sebastian flashed Sir Henry a broad grin. "No, though I'll be there when it starts. Meantime, since my stint at the Admiralty is concluded, I mean to resume my honeymoon."

Chapter 14

Would the abigail ever be done fussing? Diantha wondered as she watched her maid hang up her dinner gown and lay out her bedgown.

"That will be all, Katie. You may go."

"But I haven't brushed your hair yet my lady."

"Not tonight, if you please. My head aches abominably."

"Should you like me to rub your head, my lady?"

"No. What I need is peace and quiet. That's why I've decided to retire early. I daresay I'll be right as a trivet come morning."

"If you say so, my lady." Katie's expression showed concern as she made her curtsy.

After her departure, the chime of the tall clock in the anteroom warned Diantha mustn't dally. If she wasn't ready in time, the boys would not wait. She scrambled into a pair of breeches and donned a generously full lawn shirt that effectively disguised her feminine curves. As she stuffed cotton in the toes of the boots Will had grudgingly lent her, she sighed. Her own riding boots were a perfect fit, but she feared their daintiness might arouse suspicion in the minds of the other young lords involved in the cart race.

Last of all, she set a tall beaver atop her head and tucked out of sight a few stray tendrils that had escaped from her topknot. Staring at her reflection in the looking glass, she was pleased to see the hat hid every lock of hair.

Diantha frowned. The only problem with the beaver was its unfortunate tendency to occasionally dip below her eyebrows, temporarily impairing her vision. But except for this minor annoyance, the beaver was the perfect addition to her disguise.

Inside the Pelican Inn's private parlor, a loud rap upon the door startled Diantha. One of Harry's cronies called permission to enter. The door opened and a waiter, balancing a tray laden with bottles of alcoholic spirits in one hand, stepped into the room.

Diantha watched him set a flask of whiskey on the sideboard before advancing to the linen-covered table. An air of convivial good humor persisted as the harried waiter dodged Tom Pulteney's gesturing arm and continued on. He cleared away the remains of their repast and set three bottles of port and a decanter of brandy before the boisterous young bucks assembled around the table.

"Anything else, gentlemen?"

"You refilled my flask?" asked Harry Pemborough.

"Yes, sir. It's on the sideboard."

"In that case, you may withdraw."

The waiter bowed himself out, leaving the gentlemen to linger over their potations.

Truth to tell, Diantha was already regretting her decision. She'd talked herself into taking part because she'd wanted to even the score with Sebastian. Tit for tat, so to speak. However, once her anger had burnt itself out, she'd been having second thoughts. Her desire for revenge was childish, she silently admitted.

Question was, how to come about? Filled with remorse, she sampled the porter. Ugh! Nothing could induce her to take a second sip of the vile brew. Besides, she needed to keep her wits about her if she meant to hoodwink Grantley Spears, Tom Pulteney, and Viscount Oliver Linley, affectionately called "Ollie" by his friends.

To her surprise, though initially reluctant to let her tag along, Harry had behaved like a Trojan. With offhand grace, he'd calmly introduced her to his cronies as his distant cousin, D.I. Fraser. Furthermore, when Tom Pulteney had teased her about refusing to doff her tophat for a passing lightskirt and for her penchant for hunkering in the shadows instead of entering into the spirit of the evening, Harry, bless him, had explained that his shy, retiring cousin belonged to an eccentric branch of the family tree.

Diantha's ruminations came to an abrupt halt when Will pinged his goblet with a spoon. "Quiet down, lads, and prick up your ears."

An expectant hush fell.

"At Harry's request, mindful that a lot of blunt is riding on the outcome of this race, I've devised a foolproof way of ensuring that no one's tempted to, er . . . cut corners."

"Hear! Hear!" cried Viscount Linley.

"If I may be permitted to continue," Will said coolly.

"In other words, stubble it, Ollie," Tom Pulteney advised.

Linley flushed such a deep red that Diantha's heart went out to him. Even so, she hoped he'd hold his tongue. She was anxious to get the preliminaries out of the way so they might quit the private parlour, which was stifling.

"As I started to say," Will continued, "each man will receive six markers, each set a different colour, of course. Gentlemen, whenever you reach a checkpoint, you must surrender one of your markers to the link boy stationed there. You may proceed to each checkpoint in any order you wish. After you've turned in all six markers, drive to the finish line at the corner of Royal Crescent and Cavendish Road, where Pulteney's groom is stationed. Any questions?"

"Yes, where are the designated checkpoints?" Tom asked.

"There are four in all. The first is at the crest of Sion Hill, the second is where Lansdown Crescent Road meets Camden Place, the third is the junction of Lansdown and London Road, and the fourth is The Circus."

"Ho, there, Will. If there are only four checkpoints, why the deuce give us six markers?" Harry demanded to know.

"Because each cart must circle The Circus three times," he replied. "What say you, gentleman? Do the rules I've concocted seem fair?"

"Capital go, Will!" Harry exclaimed. "Knew your arrangements would be bang up to snuff."

Grantley Spears, the group's acknowledged dandy, jumped to his feet and said in an aggravated tone, "Dash it, Will! Do you actually expect me to drag a cart full of ice to the top of Sion Hill?"

His protest earned a spirited retort from Tom Pulteney. "I'd like to know what you have to complain about. I'm pulling a coal wagon."

"Cease blubbering, Spears," Harry advised. "We ain't accountable for the type of cart you . . . er . . . hired. If you mislike pulling ice, get another cart."

The dandy shook his head. "No time. Had to wait 'til well after dusk before I dared to snabble the ice wagon."

"Dump out the ice," Will suggested.

Spears shook his head. "Can't afford to replace it. I'm stuck with hauling it up that curst steep hill." His countenance brightened as he turned to Pulteney. "Anyway, I'd lief haul ice than coal."

"Gentleman, I suggest we get on with our race," said Will. "The hour grows late, and I make no doubt the owners of the carts and wagons will raise a ruckus should they rise at first light to find their carts missing."

"Hear! Hear!" enthused Viscount Linley, his customary exuberance fully recovered for its earlier setdown.

After paying their shot, the six filed from the Pelican. More likely than not, this will be the only chance to elude the rest and hail a hackney to drive me back to Laura Place, Diantha thought as she deliberately lagged behind.

Alas, her plan to steal away unobserved was thwarted by Ollie, who clapped her on the back and said, "Lengthen your stride, hafling. Never do to lose yourself in the dark."

Demoralized, Diantha resigned herself to her fate. The six youths headed for the stable near Royal Crescent where they'd left their odd assortment of wagons and carts.

Presently, Harry caught up to Will. Diantha saw him wave his flask in Will's direction and heard him ask, "Care for a little Dutch courage?"

"No, thanks. Prefer to keep my wits about me."

Harry shrugged and took a healthy swig

of whiskey before slipping the flask into an inside coat pocket.

"What type of cart did you manage to procure, Will?"

Will wrinkled his nose. "A fishmonger's. And you?"

Harry chucked. "A brewer's dray."

"And what did you get for me?" Diantha asked her brother-in-law, determined to cast off her megrims.

After asserting none of his cronies were eying them, Harry accorded her a mock bow. "For you, minx, a milk cart. I trust you have no objection."

Amused, despite her nagging conscience, Diantha barely managed to scotch a giggle. "Secretly, I fancied a costermonger's wagon, but I suppose it will do."

Grinning, Harry wagged an admonitory finger at her. "Saucebox!"

As his phaeton reached the outskirts of Bath, Sebastian's pulse rate accelerated. Soon he'd be able to gather his wife in his arms. Never again would he let anything part them! he vowed.

The full moon in the August sky looked enormous, he decided as the pair in harness rumbled across the bridge spanning the Avon River and entered

Great Pulteney Street.

It was just past midnight when he drew up before his mother's house. No light shone through the windows. Obviously, the household had retired for the night.

A sharp spear of disappointment pierced him. What a pity he'd arrived so late. 'Twould be most inconsiderate to rouse his lovely wife from her slumber — not to mention tactless. Diantha might still be miffed with him for forbidding her to sing in public.

Sebastian sighed. Thanks to driving straight through from London, pausing only to change horses, he was quite tired. Though confident he'd be able to soothe his wife's ruffled feathers, doubtless it would be wise to postpone their reunion until he'd slept and bathed.

Yawning, Sebastian handed the reins to his tiger and climbed down from his high perch. Propped against the doorjamb while he waited for someone to respond to his knock, he kept nodding off.

At last the door creaked open to reveal his mother's butler. With his coat buttoned wrong and his eyelids at half-mast, the servant's appearance fell far short of its normally pristine state.

"Master Sebastian!"

"Guilty as charged," Sebastian said

dryly. "Sorry to roust you out of bed, Digby."

"Quite all right, sir."

"I assumed the ladies have retired."

"Yes, my lord."

"Tell me, which room is my wife's?"

"The apple-green bedchamber at the top of the stairs. Is there anything else your lordship requires?"

"Nothing. You may retire."

Eager for a glimpse of his sleeping bride, Sebastian lit a candle and stole quietly up the staircase. Reaching the door to her room, he eased it open and peered inside.

Unable to see well in the darkness, he carried his candle across the room and gently pushed aside a section of the bed curtain.

Sebastian's eyebrows shot up. The bed was empty!

He lit more candles and searched the room thoroughly. Still no Diantha. Devil a bit! Where was she?

A sick feeling of dread settled in the pit of his stomach. What if she'd left him? No, that idea was too farfetched. He could understand if she were out of charity with him because of his prolonged absence, but surely he hadn't been gone long enough to justify her desertion. Besides, where would she go? Certainly not to her half brother, Richmond, whom she detested.

Fighting a rising sense of panic, Sebastian forced his lungs to draw several deep breaths. Pointless to indulge in wild flights of fancy, he sternly admonished himself. Instead, determined to turn the household inside out, if that is what it took to find her, he yanked the bell cord.

Five minutes later, Katie stumbled into the room, rubbing sleep from her eyes.

"My lord!" She dipped a curtsey.

"Never mind that," the marquess said impatiently. "Tell me, Katie, by chance, did my mother and wife come to cuffs recently?"

The abigail looked astonished. "No, my lord. On the contrary, they get on well."

"I see. In that case, perhaps you can tell me where your mistress is?"

"Your wife, my lord?"

"Precisely. Where is she?"

"Why, she be fast asleep in yon bed, my lord."

"Indeed, she is not."

"She must be," Katie insisted. "I, myself, turned it down and helped her don her nightgown."

The marquess threw up his hands. "Pray, see for yourself, Katie," he invited.

The abigail crossed to the bed and lifted a section of curtain. "Well, if that don't beat all! Her bed ain't been slept in."

"Just so," Sebastian concurred, struggling to contain his growing uneasiness. "Now, then, Katie, do you have any idea where your mistress is?"

The abigail shook her head, "No, my lord."

That ties it! Sebastian decided. Nothing for it but to roust the entire staff. However, before he could carry through with his plan, a loud pounding distracted him.

"What the devil?"

"Someone be at the front door, my lord."

Katie was right, he realized. Too impatient to wait until Digby once again dragged himself out of bed, Sebastian raced downstairs and flung open the door.

His astonishment at finding a tradesman on the doorstep was well matched by the equally surprised look on the irate man's broad-featured face.

"An odd time to come calling, is it not?" Sebastian asked, a sardonic glint in his eye. "Not only that, you've come to the wrong entrance."

He started to shut the door, but his manoeuvre was blocked by the tradesman's sturdy boot.

"I ain't come to peddle me wares. Be you the head of the household?"

"I am. In point of fact, sir, I am the Sixth Marquess of Ravistock," Sebastian informed him coldly.

The tradesman's face brightened. "The very bloke I'm wishful to talk to."

"At this time of night? My good man, I cannot imagine why. Do enlighten me."

"Be you related to Harry Pemborough?"

Sebastian snapped to attention. What mischief was the young scamp embroiled in this time?

"He's my brother. Why?"

"My brewer's dray be missing. I've been given to understand, he, er . . . borrowed it."

"Good God!" Sebastian stared at the tradesman. "What on earth for?"

"A cart race."

"A cart race?"

"Aye, your worship."

"Tell me, what leads you to believe my brother has, er . . . borrowed your dray for this purpose?"

"It be the story I shook out of the lad wot sleeps in the public stable when I went to collect it an hour past. Said your brother

255

slipped him a coach wheel to let him, er . . . borrow my dray for a midnight race. Happen I might never have suspected, if I hadn't shown up earlier than usual being wishful of obliging one of my best customers."

"I see," said Sebastian rather lamely, his brother's audacity having rendered him almost speechless.

"Thing is, your worship, that dray's me bread and butter. If it gets smashed up, it's me family who'll suffer. That be why I've come to cry rope at this time of the night. I can't afford to sit on my hands just so a bunch of foxed lords with more hair than wit can kick up a lark."

"I quite see your point. Rest assured, sir, that I will personally compensate you for any damage to your cart. Furthermore, I mean to seek my brother's whereabouts straightaway. Now, if there's nothing else, perhaps you'll be good enough to remove your foot from the door."

"Happy to oblige, your worship, happy to oblige."

Chapter 15

Eager to get under way, Diantha watched Harry and his cronies scramble into their respective carts. Tom Pulteney's groom, engaged to oversee the link boys, wove amongst the six contestants passing out markers.

"Ho, there, Pemborough, have a care!" cried Grantley Spears from the ice wagon.

Diantha saw Harry swaying in his seat and cast him a look of fond concern. Oh, dear. Harry *was* a trifle castaway. Her anxiety intensified as she eyed the three kegs of ale stacked in pyramid fashion behind him. An oversharp turn could easily upset the precarious balance. But it would do no good to try to talk some sense into him. He'd never listen to her.

Only Sebastian was capable of keeping his brother in line. Indeed, Diantha almost wished her husband would pop up out of nowhere and haul Harry off by the scruff of his neck before he came to grief.

The third groom called them to order. "Gentleman, the link boys are equipped with lanterns to make them easy to spot. Do not forget to surrender one marker to them as you pass each checkpoint. At the sound of the pistol, you may start." Pointing the barrel of the gun in his hand skyward, he shouted, "On your mark, get set, go!"

At the noisy discharge, Diantha's hands automatically covered her ringing ears. As a consequence, the other five carts took off before her nerves had steadied. In a game attempt to make up for the lost seconds, she urged the piebald hitched to the milk cart onto Upper Church, turning left a block later. She drove down Crescent Lane to Cavendish Road, where she veered right. Soon after, she spotted coach lanterns illuminating the wagons. Grantley Spears, who was driving the ice wagon, was in the lead with Tom Pulteney's coal wagon just a short distance behind. Realising the dandy had just begun the steep climb up Sion Hill, Diantha's spirits lifted. Despite her missish reaction at the start, the shortcut she'd taken had made up for lost time.

As for Spears, reasoning that it only made sense to tackle the most daunting checkpoint first, he'd made straight for the steepest hill. Now, hearing the ominous rumble of approaching cart wheels, he glanced back over his shoulder and swore. Pulteney's coal wagon was too close to be borne. Even more vexing, Harry's shy cousin was just a little behind Tom. Nothing for it but to apply the whip, he decided. Unhappily, despite his efforts, just past the crest of the hill, Pulteney drew abreast.

"Damn your eyes, Tom!" he cried, shaking his fist impotently as the coal wagon rolled past.

Choking on Pulteney's dust, Grantley gave the link boy a red marker, noting he already had Pulteney's green in his possession. About to set off, Spears was stunned to see Pulteney pull over and stop.

"What the devil are you about, Tom?"

"Thought I'd blow a cloud. Poor nag?"

Spears snorted. "Creature's not fit to make glue."

"Pity. Tell you what. When he gets his wind back, you go first. I'll hang back for a bit."

"Are you all about in the head? Why do that?"

Pulteney shrugged. "Evens the odds."

Spears broke into a grin. "Decent of you, Tom."

Alerted by a rumble of wheels, both youths eyed the apex of Sion Hill as Diantha drove the milk cart over the top. While she paused to hand her blue marker to the link boy, Spears once again took the lead.

He raced downhill at a smart pace until he sensed the wagon was bowling along faster than was prudent. Pulling hard on the reins, he applied the wheel brakes, which gave off painful squeals as the wagon gradually slowed. However, just as he was about to congratulate himself that he was no longer rolling along out of control, directly behind he heard a heavy rumble followed by an ominous squeal. Craning his neck, he was alarmed to see sparks shooting from the coal wagon's wheels as Pulteney applied the brakes in a vain attempt to slow the swiftly moving vehicle.

Spears opened his mouth to shout a warning just as Pulteney's wagon ploughed into the back of his. Though both agile young drivers managed to jump clear, the tangled carts rolled and tumbled down the steep incline until finally coming to rest in a ruinous heap at Camden Place junction. Exchanging a guilty look, the youths raced pell-mell downhill to free the terrified horses from the traces.

Having learnt a lesson from their error of judgement, Diantha exercised great caution as she proceeded down Lansdown Crescent. Spotting the link boy's lantern, she gave him her second blue marker. Drawing as close to where the wagons lay in shambles as she dared, she was relieved to find that the youths had succeeded in cutting the draft horses loose.

"How are they?" she asked, careful to deepen the register of her husky voice.

Spears, who'd been inspecting the horses' hocks and cannons, rose. "Like Pulteney and me, they sustained a few bruises, but nothing serious."

"Splendid. May I be of assistance?"

"Decent of you, but we've the matter well in hand," Spears responded.

Pulteney peered intently up the sharp incline that had proved so disastrous. "I can see more than one lantern at the hill's crown. Someone's hot on your heels, lad. Suggest you get a move on while you still have an edge."

Satisfied her services weren't needed, Diantha didn't linger to argue the point. Anxious to maintain her lead, she took off in a flurry that set the milk cans clanging.

Nevertheless, by the time she reached

London Road, the foreboding sound of fast-turning wheels close behind confirmed that the other contenders were narrowing the gap.

Reasoning that every second counted, instead of coming to a full stop, Diantha merely slowed her cart as she tossed her third blue marker toward the waiting lad. Miraculously, the link boy caught it. Grinning, he held it aloft in a wordless gesture of affirmation. Flashing him a grateful smile, she urged the piebald to a trot.

Indeed, as the cart bowled along Bennet bound for The Circus, no longer did she hear the sound of revolving cartwheels. A sense of exhilaration filled her. However, when she reached the last checkpoint, she saw Viscount Linley pulling away and her heart plummeted. Dash it all! Where had he come from?

As she handed over her fourth marker, she said glumly, "I collect Linley's in the lead."

"Iffen you mean the cove with the tallow chandler's cart, not by a long shot," said the link boy, "he ain't been to the top of Sion Hill yet."

"Famous!" Diantha exclaimed.

Recalling the tortuous climb, she was all but certain she'd be able to circle The

Circus the required three times before the viscount was halfway to the top. With Ollie out of the running and two carts smashed near Camden Place, that left only Harry and Will to worry about.

Diantha knit her brow. It must have been their carts she'd heard in hot pursuit scant minutes ago. What on earth had held them up? she wondered as she made her first lap round The Circus.

Sebastian was riding his stallion up Belmont when he sighted the milk cart pass under a gas lantern as it entered Bennet. He did not recognize the lad wearing a beaver, but desiring to know the present whereabouts of Harry and Will — and possibly Diantha — he urged his horse to a canter.

However, upon hearing the clamour of another vehicle as he was about to turn into Bennet, Sebastian eased back on the reins and glanced over his shoulder. Devil a bit!

There came Harry tooling along in a brewer's dray.

Frowning, Sebastian wheeled his horse round and planted his mount in the middle of the street. His quick manoeuvre forced his brother to a dead halt.

"Sebastian?" Harry peered at him, his surprise evident. "Thought you were in London."

"I was."

"What brings you abroad at this hour?"

"You do, looby. Where's Will?"

Harry shrugged. "Silly nodcock tried to inch past me. Never should have attempted it. Too cowhanded by far!"

"Don't try my patience. Answer my question."

"I am," Harry insisted, sulkily. "One of the kegs rolled off the back of the dray. Will tried to skirt it. Ended up ditched."

"I see. And where's Diantha?"

"Di? What makes you think —"

"Don't try to gammon me!" Sebastian warned, his tone harsh.

Wisely, Harry caved in. "No need to cut up nasty. My guess is she's circling The Circus. Can't miss her. Driving a milk cart."

To have his worse fears realised was almost too much for Sebastian to cope with. He glared at his brother. "By God, hafling, if my wife suffers any hurt as a result of this skipbrained escapade, I'll cut out your liver and feed it to the fishes!"

Harry visibly paled. "See here, I tried to talk Di out of coming, but —"

"No excuses!" Sebastian growled. "Skip off home."

"In the middle of the race?" he asked incredulously.

"Precisely! You, boyo, are out of the running."

"But, Sebastian, I've a lot of blunt riding on . . ." One glance at his brother's livid face and Harry's voice died.

"Collect Will and return the carts," the marquess stated tersely. "Both of you report to me in the library tomorrow morning at eleven sharp. Do you understand me?"

"Yes, sir," Harry mumbled, his earlier bluster gone.

With a curt nod, Sebastian rode off bound for Bath Circus. But when he arrived there, he saw no sign of his wife. However, close questioning of the link boy bore fruit. Diantha had completed the required three laps and was headed towards the finish line at the far end of Royal Crescent. Hoping to head her off, he was once again disappointed when he didn't overtake her en route. Confound it! Where the deuce was she?

Riding on, Sebastian was slightly encouraged when he saw a lantern flicker at the apex of the curved street. Soon after, he caught a brief glimpse of the milk cart. Spurring the stallion to a gallop, he ruthlessly narrowed the distance between them. However, as he drew abreast, he was annoyed to see that the beaver she wore was tilted forwards, exposing a few dark curls at the nape of her neck.

In one quick, lithe motion, he leaned forwards with the intention of plucking the reins from her grasp.

Divining his objective, Diantha deftly eased the cart to the left. However, although her manoeuvre thwarted Sebastian's attempt — to Diantha's dismay — she felt her top hat begin to slide. Much as she longed to reclaim it before it fell, it was imperative that she keep a firm grip on the reins.

"Damnation!" Sebastian exclaimed as he, too, watched the beaver she'd worn hit the ground and begin to roll. Its loss was serious. Without her disguise, even the meanest intelligence would soon realize she was a female. He must prevent her from crossing the finish line!

Expression grim, Sebastian redoubled his efforts. Once again, he made a grab for her reins. This time, Diantha found herself at *point non plus*. Since the cart was already in danger of breeching the shoulder, she dare not veer farther left. Besides, Sebastian already looked cross as two sticks, and she didn't wish to sink further into his black books.

Sebastian grasped the reins tightly and brought the draft horse to a screeching halt. Expression enigmatic, he scanned her appearance from head to toe. Diantha's cheeks flamed. She must look like the veriest hoyden.

"Sebastian, I . . ."

"Hold your tongue, madam. We'll speak of this further once we reach home. Wait here."

He galloped up alongside the rolling beaver and, leaning over, scooped it off the street. Returning, he presented it to Diantha and said curtly, "Here. Put this on."

Sebastian waited while she donned it and tucked in her hair. "That's better. I must have a word with the chap stationed at the finish line. Don't budge."

Urging his mount forwards, Sebastian hailed the groom. After arranging for the cart's return, he added a generous tip to ensure the lackey kept a still tongue.

Riding back to Diantha, he lifted her off the seat of the milk cart and placed her be-

fore him on his stallion. Diantha gave a resigned sigh. However, as the horse set off,
she tossed a wistful glance back over her
shoulder. It did seem a pity that victory
had been snatched from her grasp within a
hairsbreadth of the finish line.

To Sebastian, his wife seemed feather
light as he carried her up a flight of stairs
and into her bedchamber. Once inside, he
was loath to release her. The memory of
watching her drive the purloined milk cart
in a reckless neck-or-nothing style still
haunted him. He grimaced. It didn't bear
thinking of.

"Set me down," Diantha said quietly.

Reluctantly, he complied. "I suppose you
know you're in for a scold."

"Oh, don't be such a stick! It was a famous lark."

Anger — partially assuaged while he'd
held her in his arms — rekindled.
Sebastian glared at her coldly. "With a keg
of ale smashed to splinters and a ditched
fishmonger's cart, I doubt their owners will
agree."

Sebastian was right to call her to book,
she silently conceded. Appropriating the
property of honest tradesmen was a callous
act. Her mistake was in allowing herself to

become so caught up in her own hurt feelings that she'd neglected to examine the moral aspects of their caper. Consumed with guilt, Diantha turned away.

Sebastian stared at her slumped shoulders. He wanted to take her in his arms, to absorb some of her pain, but the issues at stake were too serious to be brushed aside.

His tone was gruff when he again spoke. "Besides, you ought to have a care for your own neck."

Put on her mettle, Diantha spun round to face him. "Stuff! I drove to the inch."

Furious because her indifference to her own safety was still giving him cold chills, he thundered, "How dare you take part in such a caperwitted scheme? Such behaviour is childish."

The truth hurt. Tears stung at the back of her eyes. Diantha blinked hard to keep them from spilling. Sebastian, still on his high ropes, didn't notice.

"In future, madam, I would appreciate it if, before you act, you spare some thought to *your* reputation and *my* consequence? I have an aversion to the idea of *my* wife becoming the latest *on-dit*."

Diantha flinched but made a quick recovery. "Ah, there's the rub. It is not *my* reputation but *yours* that concerns you," she taunted. "And while we are being candid, if you truly wish to avoid being the subject of the latest tittle-tattle, perhaps you and your mistress will have the goodness to behave with more discretion in public."

"Mistress? I have no mistress!"

"Ha! Don't you dare try to hoodwink me. I'm not as gullible as you think."

Recalling Honoria's wanton conduct at the Leicester ball, he flushed. That the tale had travelled all the way to Bath seemed incredible. However, there was no denying someone, no doubt bent on fomenting mischief, had seen fit to inform his wife.

Taking a deep breath, Sebastian deliberately gentled his voice. "My dear, regardless of what you may have heard, I did not resume my liaison with Lady Fitzwilliam."

"Pray spare me your lies. 'Tis outside of enough that you dared to forbid me the pleasure of singing at Octagon Chapel while the gossipmongers will be feasting on *your* conduct for months."

"Diantha, I'm telling you the truth. The tattlebaskets have spun that tale linking me with Lady Fitzwilliam out of empty air. As to singing in public, truly, my dear, it's not all the thing."

"Fiddlestick! Before I agreed to appear,

your mama assured me, since a number of other ladies have sung there in the past, my conduct would be considered unexceptional."

Sebastian frowned. "True in most instances. However, your situation is . . . unique."

"You mean because I'm baseborn? That hardly seems fair."

"Fair or not, for your own sake, I cannot permit it."

Diantha felt as if the walls were closing in on her from all sides. "You don't understand. I need to sing."

"Sing if you must . . . only not in public."

Her eyebrows shot up. "Does this edict extend to the drawing-room?"

"No, but . . . to be frank, I'd prefer you didn't sing there either."

"Sir, what you propose is infamous! My voice is better than those of many ladies who entertain their friends."

"I'm sorry, Diantha. My mind is made up."

She stamped her foot. "So is mine! I shall sing at Octagon Chapel, so there!"

"By damned, you will not!" he shouted. "Listen to me, you little fool! I love you too much to let you rake up that old scandal."

271

Diantha stared at him. "What scandal?"

"Never mind," he said hastily. "It is best left dead and buried."

"What scandal?" she repeated huskily.

"I won't tell you. Trust me, sweetheart. I can't bear to see you hurt."

"Tell me," she insisted. "I won't have any peace until you do."

He threw up his hands. "So be it! If you will have the truth with no bark on it, the reason I forbade you to sing in public is that your mother did."

"And you consider that scandalous?"

"Of course not! Maria Fraser had an exquisite voice. 'Tis the circumstances surrounding her death that the gossips feasted upon for months." He threw her a troubled look. "Diantha, are you certain you wish to hear this? The details are sordid."

"Tell me."

Her implacability stirred his anger. "Very well, since you insist," he said acidly. "On the night your mother died, she attended the opera at Covent Garden with your father. Unfortunately, he was summoned to the Admiralty on an urgent matter before the performance ended.

"She was waiting for her carriage when a deranged man stepped from the crowd and shot her in the head with a pistol. She died instantly."

The expression in Diantha's was that of a wounded fawn. "But that is tragic. Wherein lies the scandal?"

Sebastian's golden gaze mirrored deep regret. "I'd give anything to spare you this."

"Tell me," she whispered urgently.

He sighed. "Maria's character was vilified in the newspapers and in the drawing-room. You see, the scandalmongers were determined to believe the worst of her. I'm afraid they assumed she was having an affair with the man who killed her while living under your father's roof."

Diantha felt numb all over. "What happened to him?"

"He was hanged."

"My father? Did he believe the gossip?"

"No, but . . . he was never quite himself afterwards. He became something of a recluse."

Tears welled in her eyes. "No wonder he sent me to school in Kent."

"He wished to shield you, just as I did." Sebastian gave a bitter laugh. "So much for good intentions."

"Yes," Diantha agreed sadly. Then, steeling herself against the flood of tears that threatened to overset her, she said, "If you don't mind, I'd like to retire."

Sebastian reached out but did not touch her. "Are you certain, dearest? I'd prefer to stay and comfort you."

The tears she'd been so determined not to shed began to fall. She dare not turn around, else he'd insist on staying. She couldn't bear to be pitied.

"It is thoughtful of you, but, truly, I'd prefer to be alone for a bit."

Defeated, Sebastian let his arms drop to his sides. "As you wish. I'll send Katie to help you undress."

Chapter 16

The imposing clock that stood in the hallway had just chimed four. Wearily, Diantha lit a candle and stared into the mirror. Her eyes were red-rimmed and swollen. She felt terrible. To her sorrow, she'd behaved like a hoyden instead of a proper young matron her husband could be proud of. Small wonder Sebastian had reproached her for taking part in the cart race. And no wonder he'd forbidden her to sing. In all likelihood, the insatiable gabble-grinders *would* seize upon that as an excuse to revive the odious scandal surrounding her mother's death.

A wave of sadness swept through Diantha. Poor Mama. To have her virtue questioned after being killed by a madman was monstrously unfair. As for the tattlemongers who'd dragged that sweet unfortunate's name through the mud, they were contemptible.

Which only proved one should not regard rumours as gospel truth. Upon reflection, Diantha conceded she'd let her resentment of her husband's long absence cloud her judgement. What a fool she was to have believed Miss Stanley's malicious tongue! She ought to have listened with an open mind when Sebastian had sworn the rumours linking him with Lady Fitzwilliam were false. Instead, she'd ripped up at him like a termagant.

Nevertheless, much as she deplored her conduct, she dare not waste time brooding. She drenched two squares of cotton flannel with witch hazel. Then, stretching out on her bed, she applied a soaked pad to each eyelid. Almost at once, the witch hazel began to assuage the uncomfortable puffiness. Which was fortunate, since it was vital that she restore her appearance swiftly. She could hardly board the mail coach looking such a fright.

The very thought of leaving her husband was heartwrenching. However, it was high time she grew up . . . high time she stopped believing in faery tales . . . high time she faced reality. Sebastian did not deserve a wife who was a millstone round his neck. He deserved a helpmate with an impeccable background. Diantha knew peers could divorce wives deemed unworthy. She'd leave a note behind begging him to do so.

When the clock chimed the half hour, she again rose from her bed to study her reflection. Her eyes looked almost normal. Diantha packed a small valise with the bare essentials, careful to be as quiet as possible. She had no wish to wake the slumbering household.

Fortunately for her plans, when Sebastian had sent Katie to her after their row, the abigail had brought a tisane to help her mistress sleep. Diantha had swallowed only a few sips and instructed Katie not to waken her in the morning, but instead wait to be summoned.

Now, shedding her nightgown, Diantha donned a grey travel ensemble, trimmed with black braid that lent a military air to her appearance. After arranging her hair in a prim bun, she carefully counted the pin money she had on hand. After setting aside the sum needed to purchase an inside coach seat, plus money for lodging and meals, she secreted the rest on her person.

Her final act was bound to be painful, but there was no shirking it. Seating herself at a small secretary, she wrote Sebastian a farewell letter.

A lone tear splashed the parchment just

as she finished, but Diantha stubbornly ignored her anguished sense of loss at the thought of never setting eyes on him again.

She folded the sheet in thirds, applied sealing wax, addressed it to her husband, and left it on the desk. Rising, she tied on her black straw bonnet, drew on her gloves, picked up her valise, and tiptoed out of her room. As she descended the stairs, the hall clock chimed five. She left the premises by way of the back alley, barely missing the scullery maid, who rose with the chickens to see to the kitchen fire.

Trudging towards the White Lion, where she planned to board the mail coach for London, Diantha was only marginally aware of the red tentacles of dawn hugging the horizon. Once she'd felt their marriage held great promise, she reflected sadly. Of course, she'd had no inkling of the scandal lurking in her background at the time. But it did no good to repine. Squaring her shoulders, Diantha quickened her pace.

Sebastian, too, was abroad early. The sky was just lightening with the newborn day as he headed for Beacon Hill on his sleek stallion. He'd been too troubled to sleep. That, vexed with Diantha, he'd blurted out the true reason for forbidding her to sing

278

was a paltry excuse in his eyes. His wife's white face haunted him. He doubted if he'd ever forgive himself.

An hour later, after an invigorating ride in the hilly countryside that surrounded the ancient spa, Sebastian sent for Katie. "Is my wife up?"

"No, sir, she still be abed."

" 'Tis no wonder. She retired late."

"Just so, my lord."

After the brief exchange, Sebastian went on up to his room, where he placed himself in the hands of his valet.

By ten, he'd called on the brewer who owned the dray and paid for the keg of ale that had rolled off. In addition, he'd compensated the ice man for the damage sustained to his wagon. To both he'd offered sincere apologies and his promise to keep a closer eye on the two high-spirited youths under his aegis.

By half past eleven, he'd reprimanded Harry and Will. Indeed, the clock was chiming the half hour when he rang for Diantha's abigail. "Ah, Katie. Would you be so good as to tell my wife I desire her to join me for nuncheon?"

"Certainly, my lord."

"Excellent."

Sebastian smiled. He felt less harried

than he had earlier, possibly because he'd already dealt with the boys.

He sobered. How he wished he'd kept his tongue between his teeth. Knowledge of the scandal had hurt Diantha, and that he regretted. Nevertheless, he was confident that, given time and patience, he'd succeed in assuaging her pain. At least, now she understood why he'd denied her the chance to sing at Octagon Chapel.

In the dining-room at noon, Sebastian had just seated himself when he heard light footsteps. Anticipating Diantha's arrival, he stood.

Katie entered, a stricken look on her face.

"What's the matter?"

"Her ladyship don't be in her room."

"Not in her room? Well, where the devil is she?"

"She be gone. This be for you, my lord."

As Sebastian took the letter from the abigail's outstretched hand, she hung her head contritely. "I feel summat to blame, sir. I ought to have looked in on her sooner."

"Never mind that now. Go to her room and check her wardrobe. I need to know which gowns she took with her."

"At once, sir." Katie dipped a hasty

curtsey and was gone. Alone, Sebastian broke the seal and unfolded the sheet. Swiftly, he scanned it.

My dear, Sebastian,

Had I known of the scandal at the time you paid your addresses, I should never have agreed to marry you. Indeed, it was kind of you to lend your good name to someone as ignoble as I.

I beg you to divorce me and marry someone worthy of your consequence.

Your most obedient servant, Diantha Fraser.

Divorce her? Good God! What another scandal would do to her reputation didn't bear thinking of. Not that he'd ever dream of divorcing the darling wigeon, of course.

Digby entered followed by a footman bearing several covered dishes.

"Get out," the marquess barked.

"But, my lord —"

"Am I surrounded by fools? Leave me be."

Once certain the quailed servants were gone, Sebastian covered his face with his hands.

Dear God, she's left me. Never had he felt so bereft. Diantha might as well have ripped out his heart. In the throes of despair, he uttered a piteous groan.

Seconds later, an element of naked fear invaded his consciousness. Diantha hadn't even taken Katie with her. The very thought of the unsavoury elements his innocent wife might encounter gave him pause. Frantic now, he knew he must find Diantha before she came to grief. But to accomplish this required a cool head. Though he longed to dash off after her immediately, his hands were tied until he learnt her direction. He was giving Digby instructions when Harry burst into the room.

"Sebastian, is it true? Has Di run away?"

"None of your business," he snapped.

Harry's gaze was sympathetic. "It's true, then. No wonder you've been roaring at the servants like a bear with a thorn in its paw."

"Harry," said Sebastian in a deceptively quiet tone as he struggled to contain his rising temper, "if you do not remove yourself from my presence at once, I will not answer for the consequences."

"What will you do if I refuse? Plant me a facer? Go ahead if you feel you must, but I ain't budging. I've come to offer my services."

Dawning respect mingled with irritation as Sebastian studied his brother's set jaw. "Very well, hafling. Hie you to the White Lion. Find out if she boarded one of the public coaches."

"Will and I will go there immediately."

"Excellent. And Harry . . ."

"Yes?"

"Be discreet."

"Count on it," Harry responded on the run.

As soon as the door closed, Sebastian returned his attention to Digby. "Any questions regarding my instructions?"

"No, my lord. You wish the maids to scour the premises while the footmen search the town for any sign of her ladyship."

"Quite. Have them check all the hotels that rent carriages, save the White Lion, of course. I desire them to be thorough, but swift. Time is of the essence."

"Indeed, my lord, the entire staff is fond of the young marchioness. We'll all do our possible."

"Take yourself off, then. Report to me as soon as you can."

Soon after Digby's departure, the dowager stormed into the library like an avenging virago.

Rising, Sebastian said dryly, "Good day, Mama. I trust you slept well."

"Don't try to cozen me. What have you done to make that sweet gel you married run off?"

"I, madam?" the marquess enquired icily. "What any other husband would do in my place. I scolded her for taking part in a midnight cart race that Harry organised."

"A cart race?"

"A cart race," Sebastian reiterated. The dowager indulged in a hearty chuckle.

"Really, Mama, it is not a laughing matter."

"I suppose not," she admitted, vainly trying to maintain a straight face. "It is only to be expected, I suppose. Gel's game as a pebble. High-spirited, though."

"So I've discovered," Sebastian admitted glumly.

"Stands to reason, she needs a healthy outlet." The dowager shot him a sly look. "What a pity you forbade her to sing."

"Pray don't harp any more on that string! To do otherwise would invite a revival of the infamous scandal."

"Gammon!"

"I beg to differ. You've much to answer for, madam. It was your suggestion

284

Diantha appear at Octagon Chapel that sparked this mischief."

"Watch your tone, sir!" the dowager bellowed.

Discerning the hurt in his mother's homely features, some of his anger seeped away. "I beg your pardon, Mama."

"Silence! You've had your say, now it's my turn," she stated with a belligerent lift of her chin.

"By all means open your budget," he invited, his tone ironic.

Arms akimbo, the dowager marchioness didn't mince words. "Sapskull!" she cried. "Why should the *ton* bother to dredge up something that occurred over a decade ago when the royal scandal currently raging has all London agog?"

Sebastian felt as though he'd suddenly been struck by a thunderbolt. "I collect you refer to the tawdry tales being bruited about on the eve of Queen Caroline's trial."

"Precisely!"

Sebastian awarded the dowager a sheepish grin that shaved several years from his countenance. "Bless you, Mama, you've the right of it. I am a sapskull. Only a sapskull would ignore the obvious."

"What will you do now?" she asked in

a more kindly tone.

"Find her, of course. I'll set off the instant I learn her direction."

"Excellent!" She beamed her approval, then, no doubt stricken by the fear she was going soft, snapped, "See you don't return without her!"

Feeling immeasurably more optimistic, Sebastian decided to let the dowager have the last word.

Sebastian stood on the front doorstep of a neat Georgian structure with a small, discreet sign that read, "Young Ladies' Seminary," and on the line beneath; "Miss A. Pixley, Headmistress."

Six days had passed since Diantha had left him, and he was in a fever of impatience to set things right between them. Indeed, driving his phaeton to Kent, he'd cursed each mile that separated them.

Unhappily, while it had been easy to follow her trail from Bath to London, once he'd reached the city, he'd found himself at a stand. Sebastian had assumed she'd seek sanctuary under Richmond's roof, despite the animosity that existed between the siblings. However, discreet inquiry had proved that assumption to be false. Growing desperate, he'd been thinking of hiring a Bow Street Runner when he'd remembered Diantha's former nurse had retired to a seaside cottage. Had the minx sought refuge with her? he'd wondered. Fortunately, Diantha had once asked him to frank a letter she'd written to Crawford, so he knew the housekeeper's direction.

Thus, he'd embarked on a wild-goose chase to Selsey. Actually, although the trip to West Sussex had delayed him, some good had come from it. But for Crawford's suggestion, he might still be going round in circles. For it was she who'd reminded him that Diantha had attended a seminary in Kent — which was how he came to be standing here, fighting off a case of the fidgets while he waited for someone to respond to the door knocker. When no one did, he gave a great sigh and walked round the house, seeking the kitchen. He discovered a waif scrubbing a copper pot on the back stoop.

"Good day."

The child's eyes widened. "Sir, ya be at the wrong entrance."

He gave a bark of laughter. "Tried there first. No one answered the knocker."

"It's Sunday."

"So it is," he agreed, pulling a wry face.

The child giggled. "They all be at church."

To the waif's delight, he slapped his forehead with his palm. "Now, why didn't I think of that? Tell me, imp, is it far?"

"What a looby ya be, sir. Don't cha hear the music."

The organ music that he'd been hearing — but hadn't heeded — now flooded his consciousness.

"Just follow the sound, sir."

"Here's a little something for your kindness," Sebastian said, tossing her a crown.

As he neared the church entrance, he heard a rich contralto voice that a nightingale might envy. Indeed, the pitch was so pure it raised the hairs at the nape of his neck. Sebastian hurried forwards, eager to see the soloist. Soon after he stepped inside, he espied Diantha singing from the choir booth. His heart swelled with pride. She sang like an angel.

The realisation humbled him. As Diantha's voice soared to the rafters, Sebastian slid unobtrusively into a back pew. No wonder dearest Mama had delivered a scold. How could he have been so insensitive to deny such a remarkable talent an outlet?

It was some time after the conclusion of Sunday services that Sebastian was able to arrange a private audience with his run-away bride. First, he'd had to sit through the noon meal — a more elaborate affair than usual in honour of the Sabbath. Wisely, he'd exerted himself to charm Miss Pixley, succeeding so well she granted them the use of her private parlour.

Heart thumping against his rib cage, Sebastian studied his beloved's face. "My dear, you still look in a state of shock."

"Why have you come? You should be happy to be rid of me."

"Never!" Sebastian's amber eyes flashed with passion. "I love you, sweetheart."

"You love me?"

"To distraction!" he averred. "Furthermore, I swear the rumours linking me with Lady Fitzwilliam are false. I love only you and wouldn't dream of being unfaithful."

"I . . . I believe you."

He peered at her sharply. "You didn't before."

"I was jealous. You see, I love you, too."

"Darling, I . . ."

"No, let me speak before I lose my courage."

Sebastian had started towards her, but hearing the panic in her voice, halted. "As you wish."

"It was after you related the scandal involving my parents that I had second thoughts about the rumor linking your name with Lady Fitzwilliam's. I ought to have given you a chance to explain instead of setting such store in malicious gossip. As for Mama, she may not have been married to my father, but I'd stake the fortune Papa left me she was otherwise a pattern card of virtue."

"Just so, but I meant to shield you from the sordid affair." Sebastian sighed. "Alas, I let my damnable temper gain the upper hand."

"Don't worry yourself. I'm not a child to be protected from unpleasantries; I'm a full grown woman."

Amusement flickered in his eyes. "You, imp, are a handful. I trust you will recall this conversation the next time you're tempted to cut a dash."

Diantha had started to smile, but his teasing remark sobered her. Sebastian suffered a pang of regret that he'd raised the subject.

"My love, look at me," he pleaded softly.

He waited for what seemed an eon before Diantha mustered the courage to meet his warm gaze. "There, that's better. Sweetheart, I was wrong to forbid you to sing. I admit I did not perfectly understand what I was asking of you until I walked through the church door and saw that it was you that was singing so enchantingly. Please forgive me."

"But, what about the danger of scandal?"

"Yes, well, I've been giving that aspect a great deal of thought and . . ."

"And?" Diantha prompted.

Sebastian awarded her an engaging smile. "Since society is so insatiably dedicated to gleaning every tidbit relating to Queen Caroline's conduct, I doubt they'll turn a hair at my wife's perfectly unexceptional debut at Bath's Octagon Chapel."

Diantha's fine grey eyes brimmed with happiness. "Sebastian, do you truly mean it?"

"Yes, imp, I do."

In a burst of exuberance, she clapped her hands, but once again her mood darkened. "Suppose you are mistaken, and, despite the Queen's trial that has Society agog, someone does manage to revive the old scandal."

Sensing their future relationship hung in the balance, Sebastian drew a deep breath, then said, "My dearest love, if that should happen, rest assured I'll stand beside you.

Together, I'm confident we'll weather the storm."

Scanning her luminous face, Sebastian was rewarded by her radiant smile. He opened his arms and said, "Come to me, my love. It's time we resumed our honeymoon."

With a glad cry, she rushed into his warm, enveloping embrace. He lifted her off her feet and carried her out of the private parlour. As they passed through the entrance hall, several of the young ladies stared dreamily at the romantic pair. But Sebastian and Diantha were too engrossed in each other to notice.

About the Author

Phylis Ann Warady has lived all over the U.S. She grew up in rural Cape Cod and New York and Boston, but now makes her home in Grass Valley, California.

Scandal's Daughter, which is loosely based on the lives of the opera singer Martha Ray, her lover, the Earl of Sandwich, and their daughter, is her first novel.

The employees of Thorndike Press hope you have enjoyed this Large Print book. All our Thorndike and Wheeler Large Print titles are designed for easy reading, and all our books are made to last. Other Thorndike Press Large Print books are available at your library, through selected bookstores, or directly from us.

For information about titles, please call:

(800) 223-1244

or visit our Web site at:

www.gale.com/thorndike
www.gale.com/wheeler

To share your comments, please write:

Publisher
Thorndike Press
295 Kennedy Memorial Drive
Waterville, ME 04901